GRIMOIRE
of the
FOUR
IMPOSTORS

COY HALL

GRIMOIRE
of the
FOUR
IMPOSTORS

Published by

NOSETOUCH PRESS

CHICAGO · PITTSBURGH *MMXXI*

For Olivia

CONTENTS

✤

NOTE

This is a record of six tales—four stories that comprise *Grimoire of the Four Impostors* and two stories that document encounters with the grimoire. A grimoire is a book of occult instruction. Often, grimoires are clear in design and function as textbooks (with Latin being the primary barrier). With other grimoires, however, the teaching is intentionally obscured. Obfuscation was a defense mechanism in less tolerant ages, but this also allowed veiled communication with initiates. *Grimoire of the Four Impostors* is an example of the latter form. On the surface, the book functions as a collection of occult tales. Within the weaving, however, students of the occult will find what they seek.

The date of composition for *Grimoire of the Four Impostors* is difficult to pinpoint, although references to events in the tales date this version to the seventeenth century. However, other references to the grimoire as "ancient" preclude a seventeenth century origin, so it is likely that as yet undiscovered versions of the text existed previously. An original author has not been identified (refer to the literature of Ernst Ehrick for conjecture about possible authors).

Certain occultists (Dr. Béla Toth, for example) argue that the stories in *Grimoire of the Four Impostors* change from time to time of their own accord, so attempts at dating the book or identifying an author may prove futile. In unpublished correspondence, Dr. Toth speculated that, relative to the individual reading the grimoire, the impostor stories always take place around 400 years in the past. Evidently, when Dr. Toth translated the text, the stories were set in the fourteenth century. Correspondence confirms this. The stories in the extent version of Dr. Toth's translation *(Prana Press 1917)*, however, now take place in the seventeenth century, although there is no record that Dr. Toth altered his original manuscript.

Even if the stories change—be it in plot, characters, or language—the message in the fabric of the tales does not. An Enochian code, a chain of symbols, hides within the four impostor tales, obscured yet identifiable for the initiated. I caution against casual attempts to piece together the book's central teachings. The first and last stories in this compilation allow the reader to witness the fruits of decipherment. If an attempt is made to decode *Grimoire of the Four Impostors,* exercise proper caution.

The translation is new to this edition.

Coy Hall
September 2021

GRIMOIRE *of the* FOUR IMPOSTORS:

AN ENCOUNTER

in 1690

✠

he mechanical man rested on the floor with the small of his back against the wall. His neck, broken with great force, held a grotesque angle. In the decaying monastery, Rudolphus had become part of the rubble. I recognized the mask that made him distinct from his brother, Barnabas. The bronze face had weathered and turned green, but it remained unchanged in other aspects. Rudolphus had been here for some time—long enough for birds to make and abandon homes inside of him—rusting into the pose he maintained. His was now the shape of a hanged thief—a neck with a fold in it, chin against shoulder, ear against chest.

I gathered my mind, but my heart was nervous and quick. I thought then about Hyacinth, about her amusement at the sight of Rudolphus, a mechanical wonder, bowing courteously for her pleasure. That first night with Rudolphus seemed ages ago now. I wondered if it would move Hyacinth to see him like this, a rusted and lifeless derelict. The sight certainly moved me.

I stepped closer. The weak floor groaned. A board cracked.

One agitated pigeon nested in Rudolphus's lap while another, smaller bird traipsed his shoulders. *From a magician's trick to an ineffective scarecrow*, I thought, feeling like the eyes of a painter. *An automaton to a bird's nest.* Maybe this was the natural trajectory for an uncanny thing like Rudolphus. The witch's mask he wore as a face, a blank imitation of human features cast in bronze, had frightened me the first time I'd seen it, but Rudolphus had possessed a charm that grew on everyone he encountered. His blank countenance invited imagination. Humor and memories made for a thin defense now, though. Imagination could turn morbid. In reality, the sight of him broken on the floor jolted me. I couldn't hide it, but at least there was no one for whom to pretend, no one to judge my honor. I was alone in the monastery.

As I walked forward, my steps echoed against the stone walls and the remnants of the ceiling. I felt like a scared child, fumbling in the dark for the stub of a candle. A tremble moved my hands, though I tried to keep them still. I almost stepped into one of the holes that, like a hive's comb, pocked the floor.

Again, I gathered myself. Outside, the sun was bright. Summer filled the open windows. Sunlight lanced through gashes in the ceiling and moved neatly through clouds of dust. The birds protested my approach but fled when I came too near. A tree had grown against one of the open windows, its long branches reaching into the room. The birds went to the tree first, receding into the leaves until hidden properly. The birds looked back at me with onyx eyes.

I recall these things now, but in the moment I saw only Rudolphus, his bronze mask, his rusted, cage-like frame covered with the tattered brown garb of a peasant. His metal hands, not unlike the claws of a garden utensil, were empty. He had no defense. When I was close, I could see that mice had taken refuge inside his braided framework. The rodents nested between tubes in his stomach. When my shadow covered them, the rodents scattered, too. One of the mice, frantic with terror, fell through a hole in the floor. The others didn't wait to mourn the poor thing. The fleeing mice also left behind a brood of pink, squirming children, which gave the impression of rattled intestines.

I was afraid, but I knelt anyway. The work of eight months neared fruition, and I was equally overcome and frightened. I had traveled two thousand miles. When I was still, the moment washed over me. I craned my neck to look into Rudolphus's eyes. The obsidian marbles that filled the sockets of the mask no longer shimmered. The eyes were just stones now, dull. No spark touched the features, no *true animus* as Rudolphus's creator called his secret. Rudolphus was more an abandoned tool than cadaver, but the traits of both comingled to create his unique presence.

As I stared, conscious of my breathing in the tranquil room, I expected the automaton to lift his head, to correct his neck, to struggle to his feet and politely bow. I remembered what it sounded like when he moved, like an icicle snapping repeatedly. It was extraordinary, but a fine magician had once made this machine descend a flight of stairs unassisted.

Rudolphus didn't move, not even when I coaxed him.

Eventually, I stood and wandered into the adjoining room. The din of flies foreshadowed the sight that awaited me. In my heart, I already knew what I would see. A broken Rudolphus brought the futility of my search into focus. A doorway, shaped like the entrance to a cathedral, led to a high-ceilinged room. Trees smothered the windows here. Last autumn's leaves filled the shadowed corners. The sun broke through slits in the ceiling. With my every step, dust rolled like fog before me. Time hadn't erased the tang of decay that emanated from a darkened closet in the wall. I knew, but I had to see. I needed the closure of seeing, of knowing irreversibly. I stepped closer still.

Here, suspended from the stone, was a true hanging. A man who did not rust but dangled as a horror show of rotten flesh. In places, especially his digits, he'd been devoured to the bone. I envisioned the rats and birds and fly-maggots taking a piece of flesh at a time, creating this hanging thing like a sculptor stripping away layers of marble. There must have been a thousand ravenous flies in the air. They were large and blue-black and manic. Maggots were so numerous that their collective squirm was audible. I covered my mouth, but miasma entered every pore.

A balled shirt lay on the ground beneath the hanging man's feet. It was the shirt of another, not his own. Dripping decay had ruined the fabric, but I supposed it was a shirt that matched the one worn by Rudolphus. The cloth was so hard that wind had broken it into flakes. *Was it,* I wondered, *the shirt that once draped Barnabas, Rudolphus's brother?* I shielded my nose and mouth, and I turned from the closet.

I had found Roya Jasper, the magician. Although I had no firm evidence, save for the presence of Rudolphus and locks of dark hair now dry as timothy-grass, I knew. Who else?

I left the room, and I ran for one of the few windows not choked by a tree. Holding a crumbled sill for leverage, I gasped for air. The forest was hot but clean. I tried to breathe deeply, to wash the tang from my senses. My knees wanted to buckle. I held tight to keep from going down.

An idea rushed into me like a sickness. I turned and looked at Rudolphus just to be certain. An innocuous thing turned morbid: Barnabas the Coffin Maker was nowhere in sight. A discarded tunic, that of a peasant, was the only evidence he had ever been here. Roya Jasper had traveled with two automatons. He now hung dead beside one of the machines. The other mechanical man was gone.

It was night when I reached the caravan of Almos Toth. The gypsies had built many fires, and they had arranged wagons like the battlements of a fortress. Inside the ring, around the fires, Almos Toth's people danced and sang busily, celebrating in the old pagan style that pervaded the east. Their sorrowful voices and steady drums moved up the hillside, accompanied by the aroma of roasting meat. After hours of riding, my hunger finally returned (although the desire was fragile when my mind went back to the images of Roya Jasper and Rudolphus).

The black river ran along the far side of Toth's camp. Firelight touched each shore, but the river was dark like coal at its heart. There was no moon that night to ride on the blackness of the water. The village of Lugos stood on the opposite side of the river. Lugos was quiet and Christian. Tonight, the river divided two worlds— worlds that knew one another, touched now and again, but ultimately despised and rejected the other. Hungary was a land of deep divisions and hatreds, like any place caught between strong forces.

I dismounted from my horse. The gray mare was ex- hausted. She kept her head low. Sweat made her neck slick, and her hair was a skein of knots. I stroked her face, promising food and rest, and then we descended the hill- side together. A breeze moved in from the river, pushing wood smoke. The worst heat of the day was gone, but the humidity of the forest seemed to have followed me.

Over my shoulder, the forest was nearly as loud as Toth's caravan. Wolves bayed in the distance.

The Romani are a wary people, having been kicked around between Ottomans, Germans, and Hungarians for generations, so, naturally, an armed man rode out to greet me. He held a short sword in his grip. I doubted he'd ever used the weapon, but I had not seen his face before and couldn't dismiss him entirely. Any man with a weapon and youth is dangerous.

I stopped with the horse and looked up. "Heath May," I said. Then, in the tongue most familiar to him, "A friend of Mr. Toth."

The man on the horse grunted, then turned back to the camp. Apparently, he knew my name, but he said nothing to acknowledge the fact. There was no reason he should not know my name. I had traveled with the Toth caravan two weeks prior. He went on. Out of boredom, he spurred the tall horse. Hoofs beat the earth. He let out a little yell of prowess.

After taking care of the mare and placing her in a makeshift corral with other horses, I moved towards the circle of wagons. The man with the sword watched me again. When I demonstrated I was unarmed, he turned away. Impatiently, he tapped the sword against his leg to the drumbeat. He was very youthful, I noticed now, just a fast growing child. I made a shallow greeting, a symbol with my left hand Almos Toth had shown me, but the youth didn't acknowledge it.

I walked through a space between the wagons and came upon a low fire. The air was a thick tangle of smells: smoke, food, sweat, horses, pigs. A pretty girl, adorned with many beads, danced alone at the edge of the fire. The circle of men and boys watched, quite absorbed. I doubted their attention was solely religious. A man with a drum sang from deep in his throat, not unlike what one hears farther east in Nepal. The scene was, as it always was, discordant but mesmerizing. The girl had long black hair and Mongolian skin. The colorful skirt of her dress rose and fell, revealing bare feet and ankles. Heavy breasts moved freely under the thin fabric of her blouse. She aroused something deeply primitive. Her motion was frenzied, ecstatic, all too pagan. The sheen on her dark eyes was like a veil. One could stare into the eyes and see what one wanted.

Toth caught me watching. Perhaps he read my thoughts. He and his young wife, Cicely, made the dexterous symbol with their left hands. Although I nearly returned the greeting, like a waving Englishman, I checked the instinct with only a twitch of the shoulder. To accept a greeting here one only nods acceptance. To match the greeting is boorish, a sign of rivalry, something boys and enemies do. The lesson could be a difficult one to learn.

Toth touched my shoulder when he came close. There was gravity in his eyes, but he said nothing. I followed him to his tent. Cicely remained behind. She was heavy with child, but, despite pricks of sweat on her brow, she hid the discomfort well. She did what she was brought into this world to do: Cicely carried Almos Toth's eighteenth child. Almos already knew it would be a boy, and he had named the unborn son Béla. Cicely watched the dancing girl like the scene was something new. I hunkered and went inside the tent.

Toth took a seat on a pile of blankets. I sat on the floor. The tent was opulent by the standards of the gypsies, full of blankets and Persian smoking paraphernalia. There was an essence of barnyard animals here, too, like pig hides, and the ubiquitous wood smoke of the Romani colored everything. Toth, a hard, leathery man in his fifties with a dark mustache and dark hair balled beneath a silk hat, said in his own tongue, "I can see you found something. It did not take you so long." His eyes, slightly Mongolian, moved over me, went through me. I had become convinced the man could probe thoughts.

I hated to think I was that easy to read. In my estimation, years of nights at the court of Lady Willoughby taught me the luxury of a mask. What was a courtier without his disguise? I prided my ability. Then again, a mask to the English was not a mask here. Toth funded the caravan with his ability to read men. He'd studied the old Egyptian arts. I've no doubt he taught Roya Jasper a thing or two. I nodded. "Jasper," I said, "and one of his machines."

He looked troubled then. "Only one?" he asked.

"The machine named Rudolphus. It was in one room. Jasper was in the next. He'd been dead a long while. I didn't have the courage to move him," I admitted.

"Roya loved the old monastery," Toth said, remembering. "He often studied there." He was silent for a moment, then said, "I knew it would be there you'd find him."

We said nothing of the grimoire. It was a subject too heavy to broach. We shared the omission, if nothing else.

"When Jasper traveled with you, he had both machines?" I asked.

"Rudolphus with his bowing and Barnabas with a hammer in his hand, nailing planks. Both were part of his show then. Wondrous things." Toth reached into the clutter behind him and pulled out a stoppered cask. He uncorked the bottle and offered a drink. This was a liquid the gypsies recognized as wine, in fact *called* wine, but I found it to be swill. I knew Toth well enough to decline without offense. He drank freely from the bottle until wine pearled in his mustache. The alcohol didn't quite make it to his eyes. "Would it trouble you to know I suspected Barnabas would not be there?" he asked.

"Why do you say that?"

Toth stood. "Wait here," he said. He went out of the tent. The music and smoke came in from the outside. In less than a minute he was back with an old man in an oversized peasant tunic. The man was dark, his hair a dirty silver. He was thin as his bones permitted. Toth reclaimed his seat and motioned for the man to find a space. The old man obeyed. He sat at my side and crossed his brittle legs. He'd brushed my shoulder as he passed, but he wouldn't look in my eyes.

"This is Blasko," Toth said. He looked at the old man. "Tell Lord May what you saw."

Blasko spoke in a reedy voice. He watched the edge of the tent as he talked. What remained of his teeth was spotted brown and rotten. "The Coffin Maker," he started. He was silent then.

"Yes?" I urged. "Barnabas."

"This was months ago. In the village of Ferenc. An ugly mountain village." Disheartened by the memory, he stopped. No doubt he felt like a fool.

"Go on," Toth ordered.

"He was no longer a cage of metal. He no longer wore a mask. He had flesh." Blasko pinched his leathery arm. "He moved like a man."

Incredulous, I asked, "How did you know it was Barnabas?"

"He did not look odd. He was nailing a coffin together. I saw his hammer. It was the same tool he always used."

"Barnabas is a name in the Bible," I said. "Others could have it inscribed on a tool."

Blasko smiled. If Toth had not been near, the old man would have demanded a bribe to continue. He had that look. With Toth's glower on him, though, he said, "I spoke to him. I can be a gadfly when I choose."

"What did he say?"

Blasko raised his fist. "He held up the hammer like a machine, but he pointed it at me. I said, 'Where is your master?' He denied he ever had a master. He was a free man, he said, called me a beggar. He spat at me. I said, 'The magician. The Mr. Jasper?' He watched other villagers on a dirt path as I spoke, but his knuckles were white. I told him I was a slave of the Ottomans once, to get him to lower his guard. 'I don't want money. I'm not begging. We are kindred,' I said. 'Owned men.' He raised the hammer again, and his face grew pale. 'What of your brother, Rudolphus?' I asked. 'What of your kin?' He swung the hammer down so hard he split the plank, ruining it. Lebanon cedar, it was. I could smell the broken grain. Barnabas told me he'd do the same to me if I didn't move on. People were watching us by then. He seemed very ill at ease."

"Now you see why I suspected Barnabas would not be with Rudolphus," Toth said.

An odd thought occurred to me. Barnabas would be a foreigner in any land. "In what accent did he speak?" I asked.

"Yours," Blasko said. "His, like yours, was an awkward command of the tongue."

Fascinating, I thought. *Did Barnabas learn his voice from Jasper?*

Blasko began to rise.

"Stay here," Toth ordered. "Blasko is a magician in his own right. I've never seen a thief with a skill his equal. Show Lord May what you've taken from him."

Blasko shrugged. From his shirt (now I knew the reason behind its voluminous size) he retrieved a pouch of silver coins. He held it out like a guilty cat with sinew in its teeth. I felt for the pouch at my waist. It was not there. I snatched the coins away from the old man.

Blasko smiled wanly.

"No harm meant," Toth said. "Just an illustration."

I was beginning to catch on. "What did you take from him?" I asked.

Blasko reached into his shirt and pulled out a worn hammer. Burned into the chestnut handle was the name Barnabas.

I became conscious of my heart then. The pulse moved into the base of my throat. "Would he have killed Jasper?" I asked. "If Jasper had—"

"—Blasko shall accompany you to Ferenc," Toth interrupted. He was afraid of the grimoire. He would not allow me to say the name of the book. "I'll have provisions made ready."

"I can pay you," I said, grateful.

"Weigh your purse," Toth said. "You already have."

Indeed, I was poorer by five coins.

Memories: The Lady Willoughby's Court

Lady Willoughby gave off an air of anticipation, as if she were always waiting on something momentous to occur. She was poised for joy or pleasure, but never seemed to find either. Presently, she waited behind the long table, her hands prim and still, delicate as petals beneath the lace at her wrists. Despite the murmuring crowd that moved around her, the surfeit of drink, the pinging harpsichord, she looked bored. The white ruff she wore as a collar framed her face, playing counterpoint with her blue eyes. The lace was undisturbed, arranged like her chambermaids had set it at the beginning of the night. She had not moved from the table since she'd been led there an hour previously.

I was not dancing, so I tended a drink and watched her. She had been cold with me for the past week. Accordingly, I kept my distance. Lady Willoughby had a nuanced beauty, one you had to search for to find. You could watch all night and not see it emerge. She found prettiness trifling, and she never attempted something so low. She was too well trained for anything about her presence to be self-evident. Her father had been a courtier for King Charles before the war. She'd been trained since infancy. I hadn't found her beauty until I'd known her a year, until, like her inner circle, I'd learned to call her Hyacinth rather than My Lady Willoughby. Behind the table, a mahogany chair at her back rising two feet above her scarlet wig, she was alone. The Lord's chair at her side remained empty. She'd been a widow for a decade, and she was not quite thirty.

The scene went on like this, forced, somewhat painful to endure. It reminded me of the plague stories in Boccaccio's *Decameron*—people attempting trivial entertainments while waiting for the plague to pass. And in the back of their mind, and woven into the stories they told, *memento mori*. That was this night.

One of the criers, purposely foolish in silk pantaloons that gathered around his knees, blew a horn at the crowd.

The Willoughby banner hung from the instrument. It was ridiculously Elizabethan, just another layer of humor. The quintet of musicians let their music fade away. The crier stood atop a squat flight of stairs, an architectural gratuity that separated two ballroom floors, and doffed his feathered cap. He tucked the horn beneath his arm. He waited for the crowd to settle further, and then said, "Presenting to My Lady, the magician Roya Jasper and his automatons." He said the last word with a flourish, like he'd practiced it.

From the upper floor, which was empty tonight and most nights, emerged a man who was tall and thin. He looked like he'd known hunger. There was something inelegant, something of the peasant in the structure of his bones and in his gait. He was dressed as I imagined Flemish artists to dress, with black breeches and tights, with buckled shoes, in a coat of the same color with shining buttons and artfully spilling frill at the elbows and neck. Maybe he wanted to be the late Walter Raleigh. It was a modest amount of ruff he wore, a self-conscious amount. I read men daily, and this one had a manufactured air. He wore a cloth hat, also black, over his natural hair. He styled his hair in the manner of Charles Stuart, long and brushed, falling to his shoulders. He had stage presence, though, like an actor. He drew the attention of the room. He stood, framed by the massive windows at his back. Moonlight silvered the glass, and again I thought of plague winds pressing our domicile.

I separated myself from the crowd, moving closer for a better view. I did not know what an automaton was, but I was eager to learn. I looked back at Hyacinth. Her hands hadn't moved, yet more life filled her eyes. Nothing happened here without her knowing, so it was obvious she'd arranged for the magician's appearance. For the moment, she was ready to be pleased. Jealously, I wondered if she'd had this man in her rooms. The thought burned and stuck. It would never leave. It colored every conclusion I would ever draw about the man.

He bowed. Then he stunned all of us, even the most jaded among the crowd. "Come forward," he said, in an accent I'd last heard in Wales.

At this simple command, a shape appeared at the top of the stairs. A man made of metal, pieced together and pinned at the joints, a man nearly six feet tall and wearing a gleaming bronze mask, featureless as those in a Greek play, took a step. Astonishingly, the mechanical man made the cumbersome journey to the bottom of the stairs. He took one step at a time. There was something chilling about his simultaneous proximity and distance to a real man. He had solid black eyes that looked out on us as he came forward. The magician coaxed, like a man trying to get a bird to alight on his forearm. The mechanical man wore a shirt with flaxen trousers, both hanging loose upon his caged frame. Beneath the clothes one could see strips of metal like a network of bones.

Automaton, indeed, I thought. *A walking machine.*

"This is Rudolphus," Roya Jasper said. "Be courteous, Rudolphus. You're in the presence of society's betters. Show your manners. Rise above your station, man."

This drew a condescending laugh.

The mechanical man, Rudolphus, arms stiff at his side, bowed at the waist. His frame made a clicking sound with each motion, like a brittle snap.

As he bowed, I caught a glimpse behind the mask. The inner part of his head was a dark cavity. The sight stuck in my mind. The mask, like the masks humanists spoke of when disparaging the dark ages, a witch's mask with spikes on the inside meant to maim and torture, housed nothing except obsidian eyes. His was an otherwise empty skull. The back of the head was another cage, squared rather than rounded. This was not a trick. There was no man hiding inside a costume (I'd heard once of a magician who deceptively placed a man inside a box and called it a chess-playing device, a thinking machine). Rudolphus came out of the bow. He straightened.

The lowborn would call this sorcery, I thought. My mind even went there momentarily. I'd once heard a story that John Dee, Elizabeth's philosopher, created a mechanical beetle that flew for a stage production, and that he suffered accusations of witchcraft for the labor. The witch's mask, I gathered, was meant to be ironic in that sense. Roya Jasper had a peculiar sense of humor, dangerous for a man in his line of work.

"How'd you come by this?" one of the courtiers asked. It was Hyacinth's so-called court philosopher, Professor Fretwell. He was a fat old fool—more a salesman than a scholar. He'd placed his name on the thoughts and books of others. "It appears to be anatomically correct."

The latter comment drew a round of snickering. Professor Fretwell grew red. He hadn't meant the remark in that way. He hadn't enough humor or cunning to be vulgar, yet he had enough awareness to be humiliated.

"I constructed him," the magician said. Before a barrage of questions came forth, Jasper added, "There's another. Wait here, Rudolphus."

The mechanical man stared ahead. He did not move. I watched for the slightest twitch, but the thing was perfectly still. I wondered if his eyes saw anything or nothing.

Roya Jasper walked up the stairs to the upper floor. He beckoned us to follow. We did. I was at the front of the crowd now, astounded. Even Hyacinth had left her perch at the table. She parted the crowd and, with two assisting servants, walked up the stairs. Jasper directed our attention now. He could have said anything, but he simply pointed.

There was, as he promised, another automaton. This one, although similar in size, shape, and dress to Rudolphus, possessed a different air. There was something aloof in its manner, something of the cat, as if it would disdain the parlor trick of bowing for a crowd. It was fitting that this machine remained behind while Rudolphus warmed up the crowd. This machine wielded a hammer.

"This is Barnabas the Coffin Maker," the magician said proudly. "My finest creation."

Two more servants came from the shadows carrying planks of wood. The young men positioned the wood between two tables. Barnabas the Coffin Maker stood patiently. I laughed at the thought, but there was something regal in his posture. When Jasper bade him to begin, Barnabas placed a metal nail atop one of the planks. He had hands like claws—long metal fingers. His strength was great enough that he started the nail simply by pushing it in. Then, holding the hammer high, he drove the nail with precision, driving it in fully with a single blow.

Hyacinth, the Lady Willoughby, chortled, which was the most stunning development of the night.

Roya Jasper had gold in his eyes, and I was too impressed to hate him for it.

Barnabas drove another nail. Then another. He was, I realized, making a design in the plank, a little picture.

"An artist," Hyacinth exclaimed. "An artist!"

"A gift for My Lady," Jasper said.

"Brilliant," I muttered.

Fittingly, the design took the shape of a cat, chin and tail trained high.

"Does a Christian man not deserve Christian burial?" Blasko asked. "I was under the impression that meant something to the English."

We neared a brook that intersected the road. A recent storm had left water moving among its rocks. It was clean water, far from any village, and the sound was idyllic. I slowed the mare and dismounted. She walked forward to the water and drank. Blasko, who insisted I spoiled horses, remained in the saddle as his mount partook.

Stretching my back in the shade, I said, "I have my doubts he was ever Christian at all."

Blasko looked back and grinned. He was wearing a bright yellow headscarf that nearly touched his eyes. His flowing shirt moved in a breeze that came out of the woods. He was not as frail as I had imagined that night in Toth's camp. There was a wiry strength about him. "You speak like old women speak, Lord May. Of witches, no? Of demons?" He laughed a little. "Or maybe that is just your way in the west."

I ignored the irreverence. I had no need or desire to save face here, alone with a mongrel. It was astounding how Blasko's mood and manner changed when he was not under the thumb of Almos Toth. He had the confrontational nature of a peasant. If in England, I would have said he was bred for the infantry. "There are such things," I said.

Blasko leaned on the pommel of his saddle. The sound of the horses drinking came between us. "I have been to the land of the Germans," he said, "where they kill witches. Where they kill Romani, too." Romani was the preferred nomenclature for the gypsies. Gypsy, to them, was pejorative.

I looked back up the road we'd traveled. We had a full day of riding behind us and a full day ahead. We'd entered the foothills of the Carpathian Mountains where every stony road sloped upward. The scent of evergreens drifted in from the surrounding forest. The sun was high, and the sky full of thick clouds. Shadows moved across the road.

"Will Almos Toth send someone to cut him down?" I asked. I had, more than once, felt guilt about leaving Jasper as I'd found him. In many ways my behavior was disgraceful. Perhaps it was cowardly.

Blasko pulled his horse from the brook. "Toth wouldn't find a soul willing," he said. "The Romani are even more superstitious than the Germans." At this, he erupted in laughter. His face was nothing except corded lines beneath the headscarf.

I retrieved the mare. "I've never understood why Toth allowed Jasper to travel with your caravan. How did your people feel about him?"

Blasko sobered and wiped tears from his eyes. He eased his horse across the stream. "There was a time when we thought him a great technician. A philosopher."

"He was. What changed?"

"Tell me this, Lord May. You found Roya Jasper. That was your duty. You can report back to your Lady. Isn't that true? You can start the long journey home. But you don't. You go deeper. Why? What is it that you suspect?"

I mounted the horse. I said nothing then. He knew what I suspected.

"You suspect what we began to suspect," he said. "That he found his book."

"I've no doubt he found his book," I said.

We shared silence and rode on.

Memories: Hyacinth's Chamber of Fools

Hyacinth understood the power of pageantry and the allure of secrecy. Each of these things alone bent wills, but the mixture of both intoxicated. She'd learned this truth from either the Church or the French. In her sprawling estate, with its twin ballrooms and chapels and kitchens and libraries and myriad bedrooms, she kept one room a secret. This room, on the top story near an unused bell tower, remained closed and locked at all times. In public conversations, the Lady Willoughby sometimes alluded to placing an armed guard in front of the door, just to fuel rumors and stoke curiosity. Most guests, even most courtiers, never saw the inside of this room, but I've no doubt that, to the last of them, they spied the exterior of the closed door.

Hyacinth wanted the uninitiated, the excluded, to believe people ruled the world behind that door, but really all that ever happened was frivolous talk and the occasional sinning. Sometimes Hyacinth showed off an imported exotic from the Americas or Asia. I had tried

Portuguese opium and Japanese tea there for the first time. She'd even had a chained Inuit native from New-foundland inside the room once (no one ever knew, and no one asked, what happened to the lad after that night).

The room consisted of three couches, each with a unique table, three shelves of old books that Hyacinth would never read, and a single octagonal window (an odd flourish that would've better fit a rectory). There was a fireplace and a glittering chain of candles. The cloistered room became unbearably hot in summer. Wind sounded marvelous in the high room in winter. Sometimes rain or snow pelted the black glass.

Hyacinth called the room her Chamber of Fools.

Assuring Roya Jasper that his automatons would be safe in the hands of the servants, that they would not be "undone" as he put it, I led the magician up an ancient stairwell with a candle in my grip. The glow trembled against the wall. I sensed he was terribly anxious and uncomfortable. This was the first time I had been truly alone with the man, although he had performed at the Willoughby estate many nights by that time. His nerves were palpable. Still jealous of the attention he received, I did nothing to assuage his anxiety. Like sticking a fin-ger into a raw wound, I played with his fear. I ruined my posture, walking as though my spine were a hook, mov-ing like I'd seen old executioners move. I said fleeting things about sorcery and alchemy. I reminded him that the Stuart patriarch, old King James, had written a book on demonology. If the late king believed in sorcery, what then? What would he say of the automatons?

As we approached the door, complete tonight with a burly servant standing guard and wielding a decorative Asian sword from the collection of Hyacinth's father,

Roya Jasper was the one who nearly came undone. I've no doubt he'd been threatened with charges of witchcraft by many a simpleton during his brief lifetime. Sweat stood out on his brow. He wrung his hands.

Taking pity, I said something about Hyacinth being a Puritan. It was too much, too ludicrous. He made a face of disbelief, and then he and I started laughing. Even the servant with the Asian sword cracked a smile.

"Cruel man," Jasper said.

After telling the servant to go on his way, Jasper and I entered the chamber. There sat the Lady Willoughby. Although still dressed in a stylish and formidable gown, she had removed the ruffs from her neck, elbows, and wrists. Her natural hair, a deeper red than the wig she wore, fell upon her shoulders. She sipped clear liquor she'd imported from the West Indies. I recognized the lingering scent. She smiled, possessing all the subtlety of a feline waiting patiently on a prize.

I shut the door and directed Roya Jasper to one of the couches. He was still wringing his hands.

The village of Ferenc lay in a stony valley, with a few houses spread along the side of a hill. This was hill country, where imposing gray mountains rose in the distance, rendering everything somehow smaller. People looked like alabaster figurines in the palm of a giant's hand. A light fog hung over the valley that morning. The villagers were up with the sun, busy, working in circles for no real end. These were hard folk, isolated, accustomed to managing affairs without interference.

Blasko and I were the only traffic on the road. We had passed one old man in a wagon since leaving our camp before dawn. He had said nothing to us, passing by with a tip of the cap and a nod. His gaze had lingered a little too long on the gypsy. I could feel his unease. Blasko seemed unfazed. He did not make eye contact with the man, I noticed.

Some of the homes in the village were colorful and pale with paintings of blue flowers around the windows, but most were grim shades of gray. All of the houses possessed simple roofs made from thatch, draped in layers like shingles. Smoke curled from several yards, giving a stringent edge to the fog. From the road, Ferenc looked prosaic but beautiful, full of earthiness.

I never tired of seeing these Hungarian villages and their subtle variations. A series of white crosses of Greek Orthodox style punctuated the landscape in Ferenc. The crosses, recently whitewashed and bright, reminded me of a necropolis. A few of the crosses had little iron fences that crowned their base, and small boxes on their stem. Idols, beads, and scraps of prayer filled the boxes to brimming. A long fence of battered old wood snaked around the entire village. Unlike the crosses, the fence hadn't been painted in generations. Also unlike the crosses, the fence offered little comfort or protection— a tall man could step over the fence in one bound. The fence was no hindrance to a forest of wolves. Birdsong drifted in from the hills like a chorus. Other birds, small and black and pensive, blanketed the roof of the spired church. One dog, catching the wind of our approach, barked, and soon other dogs joined.

"It is best that I not speak to these people," Blasko said. He had drawn his face into a dreary mask. He kept his eyes to the ground. He was, again, the old man I'd encountered at Toth's camp. The mare shifted beneath him. From his satchel he pulled Barnabas's hammer. He offered the tool, and I took it.

I had been under the impression Blasko would be accompanying me in Ferenc and beyond. It was, I realized, a selfish notion. The man probably had a family. I felt cold for never asking, not that he would have volunteered much. The Romani were guarded people. I took the purse from my waist and pinched free two silver coins.

Although Blasko was not one to be thanked, he accepted the money. "Search well, Lord May," he said. "God protect you."

"You're a different man than you were on the road," I said.

Blasko smiled at the edge of his mouth. It was a knowing look. I found it odd for a man of his station to be arrogant, but there it was. "Like you," he said, "I am a learned man. There are eyes in every house right now."

"They'll peg you a thief," I said.

Again, Blasko smiled.

"So be it," I conceded. "Mind the highwaymen," I warned him. "And give my thanks to Almos Toth."

As the mare moved away from Ferenc, Blasko said, "Just rid us of the Coffin Maker, Lord May. We will sleep better then." He kept his face away from me as he said this. He nudged the horse and was off, clopping against the beaten path. I shaded my eyes and watched him go. He was a shape in the distance, and then he was gone. It was the last time I'd see the old man.

The weight of being alone pressed down on me then, but it was not an unfamiliar burden. I turned back to the

Memories: The Grimoire

"True animus," Roya Jasper said. He took another sip of the aromatic liquor. His eyes were growing dull, eating up rather than reflecting the candlelight. Outside, the sky held a purple tinge. Dawn neared. Candles burned low. I moved to the mantel and neatened the stubs. For what it is worth, I did not believe the magician. He talked like a charlatan, like an alchemist in search of patronage. But I was there as an extra body in the room, only because Hyacinth desired my presence. I felt I was close to making love to her again, so I declined every opportunity to play the antagonist. The proximity to Hyacinth made me somewhat desperate to please her. I betrayed no face of doubt.

Hyacinth was enamored. She practically crawled on her couch. Her face was flush with drink. "I must ask," she said, curling into a corner, "would it return to its true form when it died?"

I had never been a zealot, nor particularly moral, but I wanted to shout "blasphemy" at them for the turn of the conversation. They spoke of abominations. The thought pricked a kernel of doubt in my mind, bothered me in an intangible way.

Although Jasper did not answer the question, he turned it over in his mind. I could see that much. Following another sip of liquor, he grew romantic. "Rudolphus and Barnabas are not tricks." He brushed the long hair from his face. I found him foppish and vain. "They are mechanical men. I pieced them together like a clock. The grimoire would fuse their gears. Make flesh where metal had been. They'd move as they pleased. Perhaps, they'd think. Nothing would be impossible after that."

"The *Grimoire of the Four Impostors*," Hyacinth mused.

"It is a very old book. The Persians brought it to the Ottomans. I've heard the stories sometimes change, even as you read them."

"And then?" Hyacinth asked. She looked at me. She considered, I knew, dismissing me from the room. She was tired of my shadow and intolerance. I shrank against the mantel.

"I knew a soldier named Pedersoli. He participated in the late war in Wallachia. That was decades ago," Jasper reminded. "Pedersoli heard rumors of the book." At this, he laughed. "The grimoire sends out rumors, I think, when it wants to be found." He took another drink and laughed more. "He heard the Ottomans were trying to animate a group of dead hunters. I learned from him that the book is in Hungary."

"What if I were to fund your search?" Hyacinth asked. "Would you go in search of it? Would Rudolphus and Barnabas escort you?"

"Yes," he conceded. "I would be forever indebted, My Lady."

"Perhaps." Hyacinth smiled. "But would you return to me?"

My stomach grew sick. Roya Jasper was a sly and dangerous man, I decided. *What is it like to always be on guard against betraying one's peasant roots?* I thought. I nearly asked him that night. I almost pulled him aside and asked him, *who are you to speak of impostors?* I came very close to not standing like a coward against the mantel.

What a seething, jealous creature you are, Lord May, Hyacinth later remarked. By then Jasper was gone to Hungary, and the Lady Willoughby had yet to grow wary of his long absence. She'd yet to fund my search for the searcher.

There was no livery to stable my horse, so I gave a coin to an old farming couple with a vegetable garden for use of their shade. I gave another coin to the old woman and asked her to find food and drink for the mare. These people were distrustful of everything except money, like most poor people. Shrunken beneath a babushka, the old woman prayed for me.

When she had gone off in search of provisions, her husband, the farmer, approached. He had yet to say a word since I wandered into their yard. He had soft, cool eyes, deep set and close over the bridge of his nose. His skin was full of veins and jaundiced. He looked ill. He was a man of little authority, I sensed, but an amiable man. He had married all the aggression he'd ever need in life, possibly.

In a garbled dialect, he asked, "My Lord, what brings a man of your status to humble Ferenc? I've no doubt you're passing through to the mountains. Wallachia is your destination?" He looked with great interest upon my doublet and cloak and breeches.

"Do you receive many travelers?" I asked.

"The occasional traveler," the farmer said. "The Russian on his way to Greece. Gypsies on their way to Hell." There was a glint in his eye, something ornery. "You traveled here with one of the gypsies, no? I hope he did not rob you blind. That is all they know. They pretend to help, and then your money is gone. They are a greedy, slovenly people. Heathens. We like them very little."

All of you are greedy, slovenly people, I thought, growing weary. "Do you talk that way when your wife is near?" I asked.

He shook his head. "No," he admitted.

"I'm looking for a man named Barnabas. A carpenter. There was a time when he made coffins. What he did here I couldn't guess."

"The foreigner?" he asked.

My pulse quickened. I took Blasko at his word and said, "His accent would be not unlike my own."

The farmer nodded. "That is true. A far away accent. A heavy tongue. I don't know what became of him. But, then again, I don't often wander from this spot. The Little Miss forbids it. If you ask your questions at the Inn, one of the ne'er-do-wells is bound to know."

I thanked him and gave him a coin for the help.

The farmer pushed around the silver in his palm. "If you have more I may know more," he said.

I flipped him another coin.

Without dignity, he pinched the money from the dirt. "Follow me to the Inn," he said.

The single inn of Ferenc, an old church structure that had been converted into a public hall where the townsfolk gathered and drank and the occasional traveler rested, stood near a newer church and in front of an enclosed cemetery. The building was worn and ragged, with bones protruding. It looked unstable, like one inside would inherit the wind if a strong storm rolled through. Unless I was confused, the name translated to something like The Silent Woman, and I wondered if they were mock-

ing Catholics with a church turned tavern. The Orthodox could be spiteful, even with no one to hear the punch
line. The farmer simply called it the Inn.

I followed him inside. Being early in the morning, the
floor and tables were empty. Sunlight shone through the
windows, backlighting swirls of dust. Two young men
carried bags of grain into a storeroom. They did not look
up as we entered. There was a man with a leather apron
on and a rag in his hand. He was humming to himself,
cleaning.

"Radu," the farmer called.

The man with the apron started, surprised at the intrusion. His mind had been somewhere, but not on cleaning. He was a man in his forties with a small, round head
and large ears. When he looked around he was mostly
eyes. He had a small chin, mouth, and nose. As was gen-
eral in the mountain tradition, he was oddly shaped and
unsightly, grown in the mold of his surroundings like a
London sewer rat.

"Radu was the closest thing Barnabas had to a friend
here," the farmer said. "If you're generous, he will tell
you what you want to know."

These people have the gall to call the Romani greedy, I
thought. Their ability to extort coins was endlessly skill-
ful. They felt no shame.

"Radu," the farmer said, "here is a generous man.
Look at his noble face and clothes. Look at the fine
plume in his cap. He carries a sword. He carries silver,
too."

Radu nodded. He wrung the cloth in his fist. He had
corded, strong forearms, more bear than man.

"He is looking for Barnabas. The foreigner. Your
friend."

"I'm everybody's friend," Radu said. "Barnabas no more than the next."

"But this is a lord," the farmer said.

"Of what?" Radu asked.

Tiring of the game, I walked forward and put a coin on the table. "I want to know where Barnabas stayed and where he went," I said.

Radu kept wringing the cloth. He told the farmer to leave. The door opened and shut, and we were alone. Radu picked up the silver and walked to the bar. As he went about his business, looking unpleasant, I glanced around the room. It was a poor space with rot in the walls. The ceiling leaked in several places, and the stains had grown into large, open sores. The floorboards bowed. The dirt below showed through in spots. I took the hint and placed another coin on the bar.

"Buy a drink, and I'll talk."

I bought Radu a drink, a stein of warm beer. He took his time pouring it. Then he admired the froth. I found his pace maddening.

"Regardless of what that old fool says, I wasn't no friend of Barnabas. He gave me the chills. Something off about him. He came in here enough, though." Radu pointed. "He took that seat over there alone most nights. Right over there where the fireplace used to be. This was the church when I was a boy," he added. "Above the ceiling you can still get up in the old bell tower. Bell moved with the new church. It's empty up there save for bats and wasps."

"Must've been standing back when the Turks attacked," I said. I waited as he took a long drink of beer.

"Why do want to find him?" Radu asked. He wiped froth from his mustache.

I'd rehearsed this moment many times, and still yet the atmosphere shaped my words. "Barnabas is a murderer. He killed his father and his brother. He went away unexpectedly. I've been following him since."

Radu went pale. His face grayed. "Well, he's gone now. He left one night a couple months ago. I'd paid him to fix a step out back. He left the money and the board for the step, and then he was gone."

My heart sank. "Did he tell you where he was going?"

Radu started to laugh. "He hinted around a couple nights before. Said he was tracking down a gypsy that stole his hammer. He just said fool things like that sometimes. The oddest things. One time he asked some fellas what the moon in the sky was, and he wasn't joshing. Then he went outside and stared at it all night like he was trying to figure it out."

I reached into my satchel and pulled out the hammer. "This hammer?" I asked.

Radu frowned. "He ain't a man I'd trifle with, stranger. But, yeah, that's the one. Had his named burned in it like a fool child."

"Did he live alone?" I asked.

"He had a little shop. Did woodwork and some metal, too."

"What happened to his shop?" I bought Radu another beer to keep him talking.

Again, he wiped froth from his lip. "He just left it all. A few of us went in there when he'd been gone a few days. You wouldn't believe what he was working on."

My heart raced. "When I knew him he only nailed together coffins," I said.

Radu shook his head. "It was a man. He was building a man."

Shaken, I asked, "What do you mean?"

"A mechanical man. Had all the parts of a man. Had a chest like a cage. Fine little wires. Had a bronze mask for a face." With gravity, Radu leaned across the bar. "The face was dead blank. None of us have had the damn nerve to touch it," he said. "We're afraid he'll come back. Now that you brought his hammer here he may indeed."

"Will you show me what he was working on?"

"You tell me what he was doing building a man, and I'll show you."

"His father was a magician," I said. "The mechanical men were tricks. Part of a magic show. They call them automatons. They have gears like clocks. They do little mimicking things like bow and walk about." I couldn't help myself. I was breathless as I spoke.

Radu walked around the bar. "I'll lead you there," he said. "You can make of the thing what you will." I followed him out of The Silent Woman. We walked along a dirt path that winded between the houses. The shop out of which Barnabas had worked stood between a barnyard and a line of chicken coops. This was a shed and little more. He had not been prosperous in his time as a carpenter here. This was a soiled row of the village.

"You go inside," Radu said. He looked over his shoulder at a group of children that had followed us. He seemed bothered. He held a cross, a bauble at his neck.

I pushed in the door. The air was stale. An astringent odor hung about. There were no windows in the shed, but the open door allowed in enough sunlight to see clearly. The morning fog had lifted. Hundreds of metal parts, wires, and tubes lay about. There were pieces of partially constructed limbs in one corner. An arm with an elbow joint lay upon a shelf. There were various masks with blank expressions. With the copious material, it occurred to me that Barnabas had been building other automatons.

On a table in the center of the room, though, was the lifeless assemblage of a man. I recognized the shape and the air immediately, just as I'd recognized Rudolphus. This was not one of Barnabas's constructions. It was Barnabas the Coffin Maker himself, complete with his bronze mask and black eyes like stones. His face had not weathered to green like that of his brother. He'd had no time to rust.

I touched the cold, metal face. Whatever life had propelled him to Ferenc had gone. His time had run out. *True animus*, Jasper had said, but he hadn't spoken of permanence. Truly, Barnabas looked like a brother of Rudolphus now, part tool and part cadaver. He was only missing his hammer. I placed the pitiful hammer on his chest, and he was complete.

"Was there a book?" I called through the door to Radu. "An old book?"

More people had appeared on the path. It was as though a murder had occurred here. They had curious, dirty smudges for faces. It was an intangible feeling, but I sensed the peasants knew. It would not be long before someone burned the shed to the ground. They'd harden against the fear. I stepped through the door. The heavy stench of chickens permeated the air.

"A book?" Radu asked. The simpleton looked like he'd been caught in a web.

More people gathered. I imagined the entire village was here now. I even saw the old farmer and his wife. "It would've been quite old," I said. I realized then that I'd never seen the book and was describing something from my imagination.

The peasants of Ferenc were silent. I could feel their tension.

"Did Barnabas own a book?" I insisted. "A grimoire. A book of magic?"

"There was no book," Radu said, and I could feel the falsity of his words. The other villagers agreed. There was no book.

The peasants filched the grimoire, I decided. *They thought the book was valuable because it was old. They did not realize the true value of the* Grimoire of the Four Impostors.

"I will buy it from you," I said. I was a weary man then, but I offered silver. I possessed more silver on my person than the entire village would see in a year.

Without dignity, the peasants spewed numbers. I raised my hand, halting the commotion. We took the conversation back to The Silent Woman. Therein, I negotiated a somewhat arbitrary price with Radu, who emerged as a spokesman for the rabble. It was thusly, in the morning sunlight, in a village called Ferenc in the Carpathian Mountains of Hungary, that I acquired the *Grimoire of the Four Impostors.*

I left the village that afternoon and started the arduous journey south towards Greece and the Mediterranean.

The grimoire is a curious leather volume, thin as a pamphlet, handwritten in a strange mix of symbols. I present it to you as a gift, Hyacinth, My Lady Willoughby. What it will reveal and what you will learn, I cannot say with surety. I know only what it taught Roya Jasper and, therefore, I caution you against anything more than a sampling of what follows. I refuse to read it.

A caveat to heed, beloved Hyacinth, from one of the volumes in your Chamber of Fools:

> *Per me si va ne la citta dolente.*
> I am the way into the city of woe.

THE ORB
of WASP
and FLY,
BEING
A PSALM
of the
MALFORMED
MIND

❖

ot even the latticed fences of Chlodwig withstood the fire. The destruction was thorough. Three men, each conditioned to distrust his thoughts, and each distant from lucidity, stood in council. It was incoherent and confused talk. A wave of panic infused the exchange—rattled words, jumbled ideas, blasts of speech, and beneath it all: terror. Each man spoke, but none listened to the next. Their minds were out of synch. Each man, too, took his turn scouring the fallen fences, horse-trampled gardens, and ruined walls of the hermitage. Then, without shame, each man searched for one of the Protestant soldiers (Godless, fair-faced Swedes) who might have remained behind. The sound of metal—that's what one listened for. The very idea iced their hearts.

No soldiers remained—they had pillaged and moved on. Doubtlessly, the soldiers were heading towards the occupation of Catholic Munich. Word had spread, even to the remote hermitage of Chlodwig, about the brutal invasion of Gustavus Adolphus. Time would factor into the Swedes' share of marvelous bounty the city offered. With their bloodlust satisfied by the brothers at the hermitage, the soldiers had gathered and made a hasty withdrawal. *Landsknechts*, one of the hermits had said, when the troop of eighty or so men first appeared on the forest road. Mercenaries: amoral scum that pillaged to stay afloat between battles.

The same hermit, Brother Dieter, begged the Swedes to abstain from violence. He had met them bravely at the gates. A pitiful sight: one monk, a cloistered, tonsured, well-fed, and weak-eyed man confronting a troop of metal-clad raiders. He carried a Bible for a shield and nothing more. The amused soldiers allowed Dieter to beg, their mouths curling in the shadows of their helmets. Dieter stood in front of the latticed fences and pleaded, while the other hermits and Abbot Garrick prayed. *In nomine Dei*—a refrain repeated with vehemence in the chapel. The scrape of rosary beads. The shimmer of crosses. Dieter offered everything from jeweled covers of ancient books from the scriptorium to shards of bone from the reliquary (sacred bones of Alphage that the hermits brought out for a feeble line of visitors every Easter). In the face of Brother Dieter's plea, the Swedes drew blades. Even with God on his side, even with a thousand stories of martyrs in his memory, Dieter trembled. *Heathens*, he managed to say. His body shivered like a kitten new to snow. The swords fell with terrible weight, cleaving. One of the soldiers bore a club studded with nails. Dieter's blood touched the flowers and briars, and it soaked into the soil.

Torches followed. Through the fences they came.

Dieter, a lump in the mud, remained where he had fallen, hours later, even as the council of three chattered. He was a horror with half his face the color of exposed muscle, his skull opened to such a degree that mud filled the cavity to brimming. The soldiers had stomped his body.

Chlodwig Hermitage was not a place of great wealth, power, or influence. It was an unlikely target. Chlodwig was a home for, as the poet Brother Prana said, fools with malformed minds. Prana had been an elder, quite revered, engaged in writing a history of the war in which he died (prolific, he also authored a history of Bohemia that is still read). *Fools with malformed minds*, he'd said. Aside from the hermits, a cohort of mentally feeble men, suffering varying degrees of madness, occupied the monastery, all of them abandoned by family at some point in their lives. Some of the troubled had been abandoned as children. Others had wandered in from the war, cannon blasts jarring their skulls and turning their limbs to jelly. Still others had been turned loose like unwanted animals in the forest (not unlike the ship of fools set adrift in darker times). It was the mission of Chlodwig to provide a refuge for these souls, men whom society would discard or even destroy. A simple, caring group of men formed around this mission.

Only three of the feebleminded lived now. A day prior there had been thirty-one. Fire trapped the majority, the wing of the hermitage with their cells having collapsed during the fighting, the roof having caved. One of the hermits had thought it wise to lock away as many men as possible, thinking it would provide protection. Not even Protestants would kill the mad. He had perfect intentions.

The survivors fell silent. Their council ended. With nothing settled, the men wandered away from one another, starting towards the surrounding forest in different directions. The men had no intention of remaining united. Each would find his way.

The men had nearly escaped the grounds when a voice, and then a lumbering shape, emerged from the ashes of the monastery. A monk, torn at the side of his head, skin and hair hanging in a flap over his ear, the raw beneath colored by soot, shouted for the fools to halt. Unsteadily, he climbed over a broken wall, a piece of the garden complex, now only knee high. It was one of the elder hermits, Brother Baldric. He was a slight man, gray, emaciated. When the mud troubled his steps, clogging his sandals, the hermit fell.

The fools gathered together again, descending on Baldric with purpose. He was a kind man, beloved. He maintained the scriptorium. Action guided the men now rather than confused talk. Still alert for the sound of metal, the din of soldiers, the men lifted Baldric from the ground and carried him into the forest. He was unconscious now, his breath shallow.

One of the men, the largest, the closest to Baldric, cradled the hermit's battered head. The wound was gruesome. The men walked through a yawn at the edge of the gardens, entering the forest, leaving the smoking ruins to sunlight and a quiet only interrupted by the chatter of birds.

When he knelt at the brook, his head throbbed, the pain sharper than the blade that cut him. The indistinct face of the soldier who struck him, the white-line gleam on his helmet, flashed in his mind. The agony was dizzying, and Baldric nearly collapsed into the softly running water. With difficulty, he gathered himself. He had to remain strong. He cupped water and drank. The water was pleasing against his swollen tongue and parched throat. The men needed to see his strength. To an extent, each had come to mimic Baldric's emotions.

Physical pain merged into emotional pain, and he found it difficult to ignore both. When he caught his reflection in the water, an unwelcome image entered his thoughts: Abbot Garrick, without his simple miter and stole, gripped at the back of the neck, restrained; Abbot Garrick drowned in a barrel of rainwater, as if he were a bothersome rat, his tonsured head submerged until he stopped struggling. Baldric had never seen a man go so quickly from thrashing to wilted. His experience with death was old men succumbing beneath their blankets, transitioning from sleep to death with nothing more than a rattle in the throat. When the Protestant soldiers, two stout men, backed away, not smiling or laughing but blank, Garrick remained draped over the barrel, his bare knees cupped by the muddy ground, his head at an angle, still beneath the water.

You are questioning God, Baldric reprimanded. He prayed then, and he held back tears. God put him here. God also spared him.

Baldric stood. It was an act of pure will, and he may not have succeeded had Karl not jumped forward to aid him. The man took Baldric by the arm and propped him up. Herman and Werner, not to be outdone, stepped forward, too. Karl shielded Baldric from the other men—a selfish gesture, not one of a guardian.

"Your bandage," Herman said, "needs to be cleaned. You won't last if rot gets in your blood."

Werner seemed to be here and not here simultaneously. Unlike the other men, he was rarely lucid. "The comet," he mumbled. He had been fixated with the comet for some time. "Do you remember the comet? Brother Prana said it was a portent. An ill omen, he said. Do you remember?"

"That was fourteen years ago," Karl said. He clenched his jaw. Baldric could feel the tension that emanated from him, the raw anger.

"Enough," Baldric interjected. "Please." A wave of nausea snaked through his chest, laying a finger at the base of his throat. Black stigmas filled his eyes. "Enough," he said weakly.

Karl, a suspicious soul, moved Baldric from Herman and Werner. Having secured his niche, he wanted no one to infringe. Such had always been his way, especially at the hermitage with his section of the garden (his carefully tended radishes). Karl had lived at Chlodwig nearly his entire life, almost thirty-three years. He'd been left to die as a six-year-old boy, probably because his vagabond mother attributed bouts of epilepsy to something sinister. He was a large man, red headed and ruddy faced, pale eyed. His freckled hands were strong. His grip could wrinkle metal. He was also capable of great violence, never to his superiors but often to his peers. Baldric wondered if Karl survived because he had fought and subdued a soldier. The man would probably never say. He feared the disapproval of the hermits more than anything in the world.

Karl helped Baldric up an incline, away from the trickling water. The men walked into the shade of a sprawling beech tree. Large stones pockmarked the ground in a formation the peasants called fairy circles, emerging like the edges of tombstones from the earth. Baldric took a seat on one of the smoother rocks, and Karl plopped down in the grass at his side. Werner and Herman followed up the hill, unsure of Karl's temperament, and took seats on the ground. Werner and Herman had never been overly friendly with one another at the hermitage, but they seemed to be bonding in fear of Karl.

Beyond the shade, the sun was unseasonably hot for September, almost white in the cloudless sky. The leaves were still green on the limbs with only touches of yellow—it was late in the year for it to be so. Summer lingered. Insects swarmed anything motionless.

Werner, like Karl, had lived at Chlodwig most of his life, almost twenty years. He had been abandoned to die as a boy, as well. He had, he claimed, been afflicted with witchcraft as a child, but his willingness to lie was enormous. He generally rambled on and on about things, and if one showed interest the lies flowed. What he actually remembered and what he said he remembered were up for debate. One thing was clear about his personality: he liked to find a man he could follow, and he had, not in Karl or Baldric, but in Herman.

In contrast to Karl and Werner, Herman had only lived at Chlodwig for two years. His family, one of means, brought him to the monastery with a dowry of land. Herman was no charity case. He was an adult upon his arrival, married to a mousy girl, but his wife said he had become withdrawn and frightened, and that he saw people no one else could see. He saw things that would frighten him into a neighbor's horse stable for days on end. Herman's father notarized her statement (that statement and many others like it would have been burned at Chlodwig, lost forever). Judging by the gift of land, it was clear Herman's family had no intention of retrieving him.

There was never a more unlikely band of men, Baldric thought. He almost laughed, but his heart wasn't so calloused as that. There was nothing amusing in the sorry lot.

Herman broke the silence. Occasionally, he said things so deeply learned that it shocked Baldric. He was a well-educated, intelligent man when lucid. His family would not divulge the career he pursued before his deterioration, but he was no laborer. His hands were soft. Copious reading by candlelight had worn down his eyesight.

Baldric imagined Herman as a solicitor in his ancestral Magdeburg. He had that ironic weak-chinned resolution about him. Interestingly enough, Herman would also not admit his career. "Brother Baldric," Herman started, dropping into a formal tone, "Werner and I have been speaking. We wish to know your thoughts on a matter."

Baldric nodded, and he regretted the motion immediately. He touched the cloth that wrapped his forehead and covered his ear. The flesh beneath was hot, no doubt a horror to behold. He feared that larvae of what the Greeks called the sarcophagus fly would soon wriggle free of the bandage. He prayed for relief.

"If you are too ill we will be patient," Herman offered.

"Go on," Baldric said. "It may keep me from fainting."

The straight posture Herman assumed, the natural air of a man willing and able to speak, was another reason for Baldric's assumption of solicitor.

"We are," Herman said, "some leagues from Chlodwig now. At Herr Karl's insistence, we only took the forest road a short time. From there we headed north. You were only semiconscious for several days. I imagine we are on the fringe of Bavaria now."

Trying to stifle his impatience, Baldric asked, "Why didn't you seek out a village?"

"Again, we concealed ourselves at Herr Karl's insistence. He is convinced that soldiers inhabit every corner of the country now."

"I see."

"There were hermits at Chlodwig, sane men unlike Werner and I, who, Brother Baldric, talked with some belief and authority on a matter—"

Karl shook with rage. Baldric reached out and touched the man's shoulder in an effort to bring him calmness.

"—on a matter that has me, us, wondering if God would approve."

"Go on," said Baldric, wearily.

"Is this not the forest of the Lost Christian?" Herman finally asked. "We came north for that very reason."

Baldric hesitated. It was a tale everyone in this corner of the world knew, and they knew it more in an emotional than intellectual capacity. Children learned the story of the Lost Christian so early that they never remembered being ignorant of it. It was as engrained as language. Maybe it was a fever-thought, but Baldric imagined the Lost Christian and the promise he held, and in the moment he simply said, "It very well could be."

"You see?" Herman said to Karl. He smirked then. "He did not scoff."

Karl nodded, defeated. The red of his face deepened. Again, Baldric patted the man's arm in an effort to share tranquility. When Karl reached for one of the many stones on the ground, Baldric gripped his shoulder. Rebuked, Karl halted. He touched the stone with his fingertips. He swallowed his rage.

Werner, in a jarring recitation, a parroting gesture, shouted, "What is the promise of the Lost Christian?" His voice reverberated through the woods.

Herman nodded approval. "Pray tell," he said. "I want to hear it from a sane man. It would do us all good."

You're a one-eyed man leading the blind, Baldric thought. *When you say a thing, they digest it as gospel.* His thoughts turned lower into the labyrinth of his mind. *Do you believe?* Fever-warped, he thought, *I have faith in many things. I want to believe.*

In the open air beneath the beech, he told the tale as he knew it.

"When Callixtus II was pontiff, which was a time of struggle for the German people, a time of bloodshed like these times, a Bavarian miller walked away from his job and family. He was a happy, successful man, but God called him into the forest to be a hermit. The miller exchanged all he had for a life of contemplation. For a time, all was well, and God was pleased to be loved in good times and bad."

Baldric paused, gathering his strength.

"Then the miller's father came in search of him. Then his mother. His uncles. His cousins. Finally, his wife. The miller's family came searching, for they felt he was not divinely guided, but rather touched by an evil hand. What else could make a man abandon his children?

"Of course, the miller rejected all of them, but his wife, her eyes, made his heart grieve. He made love to his wife even though he rejected her afterwards. In the end, he turned her away, but he also questioned God. That night he wept and blasphemed. Unto men, God can be an angry father when displeased. When He expects great sacrifices of a man, He has marked you as special.

"The miller, torn, formed a plan to take his life. God grew even more displeased. God's anger can tremble the earth, but it can also be a patient, subtle anger. He allowed the miller to find a suitable tree, to braid vines into a strong twine, to reach the very edge of a stone (not unlike these stones or this limb above), before He halted the miller. It was the deafening voice of God that entered the man's mind. A voice, the saints tell us, heard as colors in the mind. *Torn men*, God said, *need time to think. I will give you a thousand years to ponder. In that time you'll wander this forest.*

"Defiantly, the miller said, *I'll seek out Satan if you do such a thing to me. I'll call upon Asmodeus, the prince of Hell, for he, too, walks here.* God was silent then, for He had forsaken this man." Baldric yielded to the weakness coursing through his body. The litany sapped his energy.

"It is the test of Job," Herman concluded.

Baldric nodded, and still the gesture was painful. Stigmas grew in his eyes. "Either the Lost Christian wanders a thousand years or he seeks out Asmodeus to end his torture. A damnation game. Of course, the miller followed his threat with a promise. *I'll endure,* he said to God. He released his neck from the vines. *I'll aid any whom you damn with similar misfortunes.*"

"There," Herman said. "A promise to men like us. To this day he wanders. Almost 500 years so far. There have been other men he has helped. The stories are legion."

"Some claim that to be so. Others –" Baldric dismissed the idea with a gesture of his hand.

"Do you believe God is testing us?" Herman asked.

After a moment's consideration, Baldric said, "It's a more attractive idea than God punishing us."

"Indeed," Herman said.

Karl, his face having leached the color of anger, stood. He held, Baldric noticed, a stone in his grip. He looked around at each of the men, contemplating. His hand trembled. Whatever he had prepared to say, he aborted. His mouth simply opened and closed. He let his gaze linger on Herman as he walked free of the shade. With heavy footfalls, he made his way down to the water. The other men watched, a little curious, a little frightened. Karl stopped at the edge of the stream, raised his hand,

and threw the stone down with a splash. His shoulders rose and fell with hard breaths.

To Werner and Herman, Baldric said, voice hushed, "Let him be." Thus had always been the method at Chlodwig, but Baldric had never felt as vulnerable to the man's rage as he did now. He wondered if Herman sensed his unease. If lucid, he certainly must've.

Werner had, no doubt, rehearsed more questions, but now he asked his final for the afternoon. "How does one call to the Lost Christian, the miller, for help?" he shouted.

Baldric sensed he was being drawn into the vaults of a malformed mind. A warning from Brother Prana competed with the shadow settling over his thoughts. It was an old saying. *Feed a stray cat once, and it stays forever.*

"I've talked too much already," Baldric said, declining to step inside the vault he'd opened. "I need rest."

Smugly, Herman smiled at Werner. "The devil on two sticks," he whispered.

Asmodeus, Baldric thought. Again Herman showed his intellectual mettle. In the portrayals of darker times, Asmodeus had the unsightly legs of a rooster.

A chorus of frogs, chirping in the mud down by the stream, woke him. Stiff-necked and desperately hungry, Baldric moved to a sitting position. Instinctively, he reached up and touched his bandage. The cloth was dry except for a small patch of fresh blood. As he explored the bandage, wincing at the touch, darkness and sweat enveloped him. Wind rustled the trees. The air was damp, and the moon was weak. He had not been asleep long, but even the small amount of sleep had troubled him. In his dreams, he was trapped in a stone maze, rapidly turning corners. He'd had the same dream as a child. He'd been ill with a fever then as well.

Unease from the dream made him morose, and his mind went from the maze to his companions at Chlodwig. He could see their faces. As Benedictine monks, the brothers maintained silence during the largest portion of each day, communicating through a makeshift sign language. Some of the brothers had humorous ways of describing things with their hands. Like Abbot Garrick, the way he managed to complain with his hands, inventing insults. Baldric missed that type of subtle joy deeply. It was odd how mundane the night felt when positioned so close to tragedy. His grief, he knew, had yet to fully blossom. He had talked to men from the war, men who had seen terrible things. Grief grew when the buffer of shock faded, they claimed. If this were not the sum of grief, he wondered how crippling the feeling would be when it emerged fully.

As his eyes adjusted to the darkness, he made out two sleeping figures near him, but only two. Just as he realized Karl was gone, he spied a third figure standing in the shadow of the trees. His relief was momentary. A dark silhouette, motionless, stood near. With a twin effort to not jar his wound and be silent, Baldric stood. A residue of smoke hung in the air, although their night fire was dead. The shape stood some twenty feet from the sleeping figures of Herman and Werner, and it seemed to be facing the encampment, watching. There was a small dot of light on its face, the luminescence of a firefly. As a whole, the figure seemed to be disturbingly thin. *It's the darkness*, he thought, *nothing more*. Baldric moved from the circle and, once free of immediate ear-shot, whispered, "Karl?"

Even as the beeches emerged from the night, details coming forth like bas-relief, the figure remained dark and wisp-like. Baldric could see no features in the face, save for the dot of light. He wondered for a moment if he were, like a child, cutting frightening shapes from the darkness, as if his dream had taken him so far back in time. He could be seeing a man where a lightning-shattered tree stood. He inched closer. A brave thought: *it is Karl or no one.* Again, he whispered, "Karl?"

The light faded first, pinched to nothing. Then the shape receded, shrinking like water against hot stone. The figure did not shrink in silence. Leaves rustled at its feet. Branches moved. For a moment, Baldric stood still, bewildered. His body refused to advance. He had no desire to investigate.

"Brother Baldric." The sound went through him, a bolt. It was Karl's voice, but it came from the opposite direction of the shadow. It came from the sleeping circle around the dead fire.

Baldric turned to see Karl, who now stood behind him. When he turned back to the shadow, the other shape was fully gone. The only evidence that anything had been there at all was a dead leaf touched by a breeze and rattled free. The leaf floated downward.

"I didn't mean to frighten you," Karl said. Gently, he reached for Baldric.

Baldric's pulse beat a tattoo against his chest and throbbed in his wound. He was glad for the darkness. His face was bloodless and gray.

"I should have told you," Karl said. "I was watching for highwaymen. There are roving gangs that use forest roads. Cutthroats." He lifted the edge of his tunic, showing a dagger at his side. "I took it from one of the soldiers," he said. There was a touch of pride in the statement.

Baldric didn't inquire, but his intuition about how Karl had come away from Chlodwig unscathed proved true. "And gray wolves in the forest," Baldric said, his breath still short from being startled. "It's wise of you."

Karl grinned. With a massive hand on the monk's shoulder, he led him from the camp towards the water. The quarter moon was on the black, oily surface of the stream. The frogs made a din. Baldric felt relief at being free from the cloister of the trees. The breeze chilled the sweat on his neck.

Karl knelt, keeping his heels on the ground like a Russian. He loosened a pebble from the mud. "Do you truly believe in the Lost Christian?" he asked. "I don't trust Herman, and I've never trusted Werner." He paused, reflecting. "Of all the men to survive...."

"That's a terrible thing to say. God decides these things. You shouldn't question that. He spared you, did He not?"

"Why not Brother Dieter then? Why not more deserving men?"

Baldric had no answer. One needed less emotion, more distance, to scrutinize such a thing. If one ever should. He turned his thoughts to the first question, though. "Why does Herman anger you?" he asked.

Karl tossed the pebble at a spot in the stream that held the moon, breaking the image apart. Unsatisfied, he toiled with another hunk of stone. "When you were unconscious," he said, "Herman filled our minds with stories. Cruel stories about revenants and ghosts, making

Werner nearly die of fright. He has Werner on a leash now. I knew Herman at the monastery. My cell was next to his. He is a different man in private than he is when one of the brothers is near. He talked to men in his cell that weren't there. Sometimes he talked all night. Those men, he says, tell him the stories, and this is what Werner believes. One of those men told him about the Lost Christian." Karl tossed another stone, again dashing the moon. "So he says."

"Do you remember when you were a boy, Karl, and I taught you to read? We would go into the scriptorium, and you would look over the brothers' shoulders."

Karl nodded. He smiled at the side of his mouth.

"Do you remember that small book of parables? It was the first book you read alone."

"You remember it better than me."

"I doubt that. Do you remember what those stories were meant to do?"

Karl said, "Teach a lesson."

"Sometimes, yes. Other times they revealed truths, or at least shades of truths, that were too much to fathom in other forms. Do you remember? It's like how we used to sweeten your medicine."

"I still prefer it sweetened," Karl said.

In that moment, Baldric saw a boy where this man knelt—the embodiment of Karl's tragedy. "We can never truly understand God," Baldric went on. "Not as men. Stories can give us little pieces of truth about Him."

"The Lost Christian is real then."

"Probably not as a miller, nor Job, but I believe there's something eternal here. No doubt something that's been here since we were Gothic heathens. That much truth exists in the story. That's what I believe. If it's survived this long I imagine it is beguiling. Mayhap dangerous."

"Herman says it is Asmodeus. One of the princes of Hell. He told another story about these woods. Tell me if you know of this."

Baldric nodded.

"He said that in ancient times before Christians, once a year misanthropes carried letters to an old temple here. The letters were confessions. A stone furnace with a red rooster painted above its mouth received the letters. In the letters went, one by one, burning away. Herman said the ashes made gleeful reading for Asmodeus. That this was boasting by the criminals rather than contrition."

Baldric had not heard this story, he admitted. "You suppose Herman would know such things?"

"It's according to whether the voices he hears are real or not." Satisfied with his wit, Karl grinned.

"They aren't real," Baldric said. He wondered how confident that sounded. He'd said it quickly, with little thought. At the mention of a demonic name, the chill he had felt, the fear, upon approaching the shape in the darkness came back to him. *Asmodeus.* It was a sin to even say the name aloud. He pushed away the haunted thought. God forbid he show such fear to Karl. "They've never been and will never be real voices," he added. "Princes of Hell have more important things to do than wander a forest or grant wishes or read the confessions of criminals."

But why so many stories about one small corner of the world? he thought.

Clearly, Karl did not accept this, but he remained obediently silent. Baldric was tempted to ask about other things Karl had heard in his cell, but he denied the urge.

He was not a Dominican inquisitor. The men shared a prolonged silence then. The heavy pulse returned to Baldric's wound, and he winced at the sharp pain in his skull. His eyes felt like stones. He prayed for relief. In the midst of the prayer, however, he stopped his litany, Latin phrases melting into a German curse.

On the other side of the stream, a light emerged on the far end of the floodplain. The light was strong enough to cut through an obscuring mist that hung in the trees and draped the tall grasses. For a brief moment, Baldric thought a man with a lantern had entered the field. The vision arrested him. His rebounding courage withered. Projecting the aura of a halo in the mist, the light was as small as a candle's flame. No lantern surrounded the light, he realized. The light floated, disembodied, like a large firefly above grass. It was an embellished form of the light he had seen previously. Baldric stepped forward, compelled, and his foot sank an inch into mud. The light came closer, slowly, as if propelled by the gait of a man. Grass parted beneath the glow—this and the grind of stony soil were not silent. Baldric recognized the physicality of the shadow below the light, as well. It was the same presence he'd approached outside the ring of the camp.

Karl stood. The two men, side by side, examined the orb, trying to make sense of the thing. Karl's breathing was increasingly rapid. He touched the dagger at his waist.

"Be calm," Baldric said, but the tremble in his fingers kept him from placing a calming hand on Karl. *That's no highwayman*, he wanted to say. *No marauder.*

Karl sensed anxiety like a hound. "When you were frightened earlier, what did you see?" he whispered. The tension allowed him to release this irreverent question, this demand, he held inside. It was not the tone of a man speaking to his superior.

"This."

The light came closer. The parting grass grew louder.

"What did you see?"

"A shadow."

"A man," Karl corrected. "I saw it, too. I saw it over your shoulder."

"Nearly a man," Baldric conceded. *An imitation*, he thought.

Although the orb never increased in size, the shape below became clearer upon approach. Indeed, it was the same dark shape, the same featureless silhouette, which Baldric spied by the camp. The shape did not float. It moved like a man. Spindly arms pushed aside grass. The legs possessed an odd, scissoring gait, one that could not be accomplished without the pain of bone rubbing bone. The movement seemed tortured. When the light reached the muddy bank of the stream, the shape below, rather than emerging fully, seeped back into the grass, individual stalks emerging through the darkness and absorbing the shadow. The orb, still weak, remained. It hovered for almost a minute. *Probing*, Baldric thought, *just as it had been watching us before*. The orb was not a flame, and it was not a firefly. From this distance that much was clear. The phosphorescence seemed alchemical. Green veins quivered in the light, growing from simple to complex, growing until the veins seemed to break the light into four individual orbs. Then, as if with a candlesnuffer, all four lights extinguished. The other side of the stream was a field of grass and mist once more.

Jarred, Baldric gasped. He had not been breathing, he realized.

Karl was shaking violently. His fingertips remained on the handle of the dagger. Still whispering, he said, "Your bandage."

Leached from the cloth, a trail of blood had the consistency of cold sweat against the side of Baldric's face. He reached up and touched the bandage above his ear. The cloth was fully soiled, soaked through. Nausea braided with the terror that kept him melded to the shoreline. There was something inside the bandage. Baldric was afraid to vocalize the thought, but he had to know. Something squirmed beneath the cloth. The edges of his wound moved like restless lips. Adamantly, he said, "There's something under the bandage."

Karl led him up the incline, away from the mud. Once they reached grass, Baldric took a seat on the ground. There was a tremor in his knees. Nausea moved through him, more powerful now. The desire to vomit seized him, but he resisted. "Open the bandage," he demanded. He could feel several squirming things now. He knew. He did not want to know, but he knew.

Karl nodded. With cumbersome, calloused hands, he pawed at the knot for a moment, then began to unwrap Baldric's skull. Sickened, he turned his head. The stench of putrefaction was overwhelming.

"God has forsaken me," Baldric gasped. Blinding terror bred panic. A dam broke, and emotion flooded his mind.

Karl held the soiled cloth in his hands. Fly larvae wriggled in the blood, angry to be withdrawn from their feasting. Maggots covered every inch of the bandage, as if they'd been siphoned out of his flesh. "Sit here," Karl said bravely. His eyes did not connect with Baldric or the bandage. He, too, had turned gray. "I'll clean this in the stream."

The thought was too much. Baldric fainted. When he fell backwards, his head struck the ground, opening the wound again, undoing the spot where skin had begun to suture. Maggots showered the dirt. The fold draped his ear, and it was clear to all who cared to look where flies had been depositing their young.

The world reached him in sounds that formed like shades of color in his mind, and he was reminded again of what the saints said about *Vox Dei*, the Voice of God. There was nothing divine in the voices, however. Between long bouts of unconsciousness, he listened to the fools. His body was paralyzed and numb. His eyes remained in the dark. The taste upon his tongue, whenever it registered, was that of rancid vomit.

Delirious, he listened to Karl. *He came again tonight,* Karl was saying. The voice was level with Baldric's ear. A whisper? *He didn't flee when I approached. He looked inside me. There's more,* he went on.

He follows us. I saw him watching. I want to show him to Werner.

Delirious, he listened to the arguments of Karl and Herman. The fights grew increasingly vicious.

He's good as dead, Herman would counter. *We can leave him at a village.*

He listened to Werner rave.

Hide, Werner. Wagons. Horses. Soldiers. Hide, Werner. Be silent, Werner. The din of metal. Heavy wagons rolling over the earth. The stench of horseflesh. *Be silent, Werner.*

Is he hidden? Keep him hidden.

Karl whispered again. *He promised me. He promised. He came to me again, and he promised.*

Did you see him, Werner?

Silence.

Did he see into you?

Another argument, more heated. *A village*, Herman was saying. *The soldiers came from a village. There must be people and medicine. I tell you he's dying.*

It'll be the death of you, Karl warned.

The jostling of quick movement sent Baldric into blackness again.

A grotesquely familiar odor, the acrid char of thatch and wood, finally roused him. He broke a crust that formed around his eyelids, and he saw sharp, painful light. Dirt, root, and gravel prodded his back. Baldric felt as weak as a kitten, sick in his limbs. Pieces of his body remained numb. The nerves in his feet and hands were dead. His thoughts were warped and hot and slow. He'd been dreaming of Chlodwig, a delusion of the brothers speaking while dead, speaking jumbled Latin not with their mouths but with their mouth-like wounds. *I'm dying,* he thought. It was a lucid and oddly mundane observation, like one notices the arrival of spring. Baldric lacked the energy to feel melancholy. He noted sunlight through the tree above. He rested in the shade at the edge of a village, he realized. Time finally entered his thoughts.

He heard Karl then, angry and charged, talking to another or to himself (Baldric couldn't determine which). "He is already dying. His blood is rotten. It stinks. I can't keep his bandage clean anymore. The flies are inside him. I saw one of the maggots crawl out from below his eye. It raised the lid."

Baldric moaned. When he tried to rise, he realized Werner was beside him, a nurse cupping a bowl of water. The water shook free of the walls, spilling onto Baldric's soiled habit, but he could not feel it. "Protestant devils," Werner mumbled. He continued to offer the water, but he said nothing directly to Baldric. His words were the drizzle of thoughts he couldn't contain. "Devils. Horrible men. Godless. Cruel men. Damn them. Bad men. Horrible, Godless men." Then, in Latin, a piece of prayer he'd learned from the hermits. *"Proficiscere anima christiana de hoc mundo."* It was a prayer for the dying. *Go forth, Christian soul, from this world.* He was doing his best to perform last rites, Baldric realized, but his feeble mind betrayed him.

Baldric took the bowl of water. Although his hands were so weak they trembled, he managed to drink. His mouth was parched and fetid. That he could not feel the bowl between his fingers horrified him. He placed the bowl on the ground and lifted himself on one elbow. "I'm not dead yet, Werner," he managed. *Although I wish I were.*

Werner was distant from lucidity. He had eyes inside his eyes, as Abbot Garrick used to say, and when the inner eyes opened Werner saw nothing except chaos. He kept holding his hands out where the bowl had been. Baldric wondered how long the man had knelt at his side, offering the water. Hours possibly.

"Protestant devils," Werner said. *"In nomine Spiritus Sancti, qui in te effusus est."* Again the prayer. *In the name of the Holy Spirit, who was poured out upon you.* "Bad men. Godless, horrible men."

Baldric called for Karl.

"Devils, devils," Werner went on, still offering the invisible bowl of water.

Baldric, his head throbbing like a hammer strike had broken his skull, looked around. It was not a village that confronted him, but only the shell of what had once been a village. It was dead ground, black as ash, still effusing tendrils of smoke. Pieces of huts remained standing, and lonely poles jutted here and there, but most of the buildings were in piles on the ground. It was Chlodwig on an even larger scale, the lunatic chaos of the landsknechts.

Karl came lumbering across a pebbled road. He smelled of horse feces, and he favored his right leg. A lattice of scratches marked his forearms. His eyes sank half an inch into his skull, framed with black bags. He looked spectral. He pulled Werner up, shoved the smaller man aside, and then knelt in his place. "Yes, Brother Baldric?"

Baldric gathered the strength to speak. The effort brought blackness to his eyes. "How long have I been out?" he asked.

"Two days and a night," Karl said. "It's good to hear you speak again. I was worried you would not."

"What is this place?"

Karl shook his head. "A village. Nothing now. We came here for medicine. But just look."

"I saw," Baldric said.

"Not at the houses. Look at the field behind you."

Baldric craned his neck, turning. His joints felt like stone. It took a moment for his mind to fully comprehend the image before him. As a defense, his mind would not accept the sight at first. The vision became real in layers. Sharp stakes had been planted in the ground. Ripened, flaccid bodies, broken-backed, jaws agape, crowned the poles. Impaled bodies. There were women and children among the men. Hair, dry as chaff, moved with the breeze. Acquiescing to a morbid drive, he counted sixteen. Sixteen bodies arrayed, sliding down the pikes aided by nothing except their weight. Some of the bodies had descended more than others, and stakes protruded from several abdomens. Ravens and hawks darted in from the trees, carrion in their talons. Flies hovered in dense clouds. It was a garden of the dead. Baldric said a prayer, and then he turned his back on the scene. He never wanted to look upon it again. His eyes were hot with tears.

After a moment's silence, Karl said, "Herman is gone." He was oddly composed. Something had shifted in his demeanor. His anxiety was less prevalent. His rage had subsided. He struck Baldric, not as the child in the scriptorium, but as a normal man.

"What happened to him?" Baldric asked.

"He left us." At this, Karl looked away.

A sick feeling grew inside Baldric. "Did you?"

Karl stared at something in the distance, maybe nothing, and he said nothing at first. He shook his head slightly as he stood. Then, as if he had debated an urge to reveal, he said, "The Lost Christian took care of Herman."

Poor Herman, Baldric thought. He remembered how Karl had stared at Herman, how he'd gripped a stone in his hand as he did so. Regardless, he was in no position to admonish the man before him. What could he say to the one who had borne his dead weight for so long? Karl was the reason he lived. Would Herman have done the same? "The Lost Christian?" Baldric asked.

Karl nodded, and a look of fervor, like that of a zealot, passed as a shadow across his face. Baldric then understood the illusion of Karl's sanity: he believed he was sane. "You saw him, Brother Baldric. You saw him twice."

Werner, who had shuffled in a circle around the men, came near again. "I, too," he shouted. "I saw him twice."

"He had no hand in that, did he?" Baldric motioned over his shoulder at the impaled villagers.

"Landsknechts," Karl said. "We had to hide from them, we had to hide you, on the road. There were as many as thirty of them. They had barrels of gunpowder. They were coming from this direction with wagons and horses."

"Wearing armor," Werner added. "Protestant devils. Horrible, Godless men."

That much Baldric could believe.

Karl searched for doubt. "We can summon him. I've asked him to heal you. He likes Protestants no more than us. He's intrigued that you're a man of God. He was above you once when you slept. He looked inside you." Karl wrung his hands. They were, Baldric noticed, hard with dirt and blood, and they were nervous.

"How do you propose to summon him?"

"In the same manner the hermits brought favor to Chlodwig," Karl said. "A passion play." This was a proud admission, an accomplishment. *I have encountered a problem, and I've thought my way through it*, he seemed to say. *Is that not sanity?*

Baldric reclined on the ground. He drew a deep, shaky breath. His exhaustion was thorough. *There is nothing good in this,* he thought. *You're in the land of the mad, and you have no power to leave.* He prayed for God to take his life, but still he went on breathing.

"The Crucifixion," Karl said.

Baldric stared at the sky. The stench of decayed flesh mixed with the charred village, and he wondered if he smelled the villagers or the festering wound above his ear. That was the world in which he lived—a world in which that quandary could occur to a man. He prayed for death. Not unlike the miller in the Lost Christian tale, he begged. It was not histrionics that moved him to do so. It was the soul-wrenching frustration of seeing what men could be when there was no need for decorum.

"No more medicine in the whole world," Werner was saying. "We've looked for you, Brother Baldric. There was not even fresh dead from which to gather blood."

"The Lost Christian will heal you," Karl said.

Baldric stopped his prayer. "At what cost?" he asked.

Karl did not answer. "Come," he said. At that, he scooped Baldric from the ground, cradling the hermit in his arms. "We'll summon while you're conscious. Come, Werner. It is time."

Any movement was agony, and the jostle of being carried nearly made Baldric faint. Again, he prayed for God to take his life, he prayed with deep sincerity, but God did not answer. *Another damnation game,* he thought, *with God watching through the smoke of war.* He then did something he hadn't since childhood. He forgave himself for trying to understand the omnipotent being that ruled over his universe. Delirium was to blame, perhaps, but it amounted to the rejection of a lifetime of training. The perilous terrain of the thought gave new meaning to the Lost Christian parable.

Karl carried him away from the villagers, through the ashes and mud of the village street, toward the thin tributary of a river. It was dry enough that the shoreline was very long, and rocks jutted from the slow water. This was one of many arteries that ran through this section of countryside. Hundreds of villages abutted these tributaries. The landsknechts would never run out of victims—the soldiers may as well have been sent by Herod to slaughter the Holy Innocents.

Karl stomped through the shallow water, making use of the stones when he encountered them. Obviously, repetition had made him familiar with the crossing. He squelched through the mud on the other side. Here a patch of forest began, an incline rising, leveling, and then turning into a large hill. Trees blotted out the sunlight. The air cooled. The leaves, Baldric noticed, had finally begun to turn yellow.

Karl placed him on the ground. Baldric was still looking at the leaves, hoping the vision of autumn would merge into an epiphany, when Karl took him by the chin and directed his eyes. "Look here," he demanded.

Baldric looked.

On a rock outcropping, two stout pieces of wood, no doubt salvaged from the burned village, had been hammered together in the shape of an X against the thick trunk of an oak. Herman, with his jaw stretched and mouth wide, had been nailed with vigor to the boards. Black iron studded the muscles of his arms and legs. More grotesquely, nails pierced the sides of his neck, stretching the skin at his throat taut and keeping his head facing outward rather than downward. Between swaths of dried blood, Herman's skin looked like graying wax. A single wasp crawled along his lips. River rats had chewed off his toes, leaving bones like a line of broken teeth.

"You would kill me like this, Karl?" Baldric asked. If he had possessed the strength, he would've stood and fought, but his hands and feet were still numb, his body so close to death the action would be useless. He could only ask pathetic questions from the ground. He didn't even have the strength to deny the urge to do that.

Karl furrowed his brow. He looked around until he found a large stone on the ground. He picked it up. "Werner," he said. "Come here."

"Please," Baldric said. He wept. "Be merciful."

Karl placed his hand on the monk's shoulder. His pale eyes met with those of the monk. Tenderly, he said, "I'd never hurt you. Be calm."

Werner came closer. "Devils," he was shouting. "Horrible, Godless men." He'd been talking so ceaselessly that white foam gathered at the corners of his mouth.

Karl gripped the stone, making his fist into a club. Werner went to his knees in front of Herman, like a priest before the altar, beginning another snippet of prayer he'd absorbed from the hermitage. *"In nomine Iesu Christi Filii Dei (In the name of Jesus Christ, Son of the living God)."* He struggled to remember, then went on. *"Qui pro te passus est (Who suffered for you)."*

Karl swung downward, striking Werner at the back of his skull. The blow sent the madman to the ground, planting his face against the dirt. He seized and urinated. His left arm curled into a brain-dead letter. Where his skull had caved, his dark, curly hair grew wet with blood. The blood oozed with the beat of his heart. For a moment, Karl stood over him, blank friction cast on his face. Werner moaned. He tried to form words, yet nothing except the moans issued from his throat. Karl placed his knee in the man's back, stilling his convulsing form, and then he brought the stone down several more times. Werner's legs stopped gyrating. The bashing was meticulous and cold, a series of efficient strikes. When the skull opened, which it did on the second blow, blood showered Karl's chest and arms and spotted Herman's chewed feet. With the fourth blow, Werner ceased moaning. The sound was that of a rotten gourd meeting stone. His brain was gray.

Karl turned. His face was emotionless under the spotting of blood. "He thought it would be you rather than him," he remarked. "He was willing."

Baldric prayed for relief, to faint away, but he could not find it. He had to look. Karl tossed away the macabre stone, covered now in flesh and hair. He flexed his knuckles, then wiped away blood on his tunic. "Watch," he said.

Numbness spread from Baldric's limbs into the rest of his body. "You're mad," he managed to say. His lips, too, had begun to numb, to paralyze.

Karl shook his head. "No. With Herman, the Christian cured me of that. Now he'll cure you."

With muddled, slurring speech, Baldric said, "No Christian would do such a thing. Lost or not."

"Watch," Karl demanded. Forcefully, he took Baldric by the chin. He pinched the man's face and turned it towards Herman.

Three wasps now crawled on the waxen face. A fourth emerged from between Herman's lips. A fifth emerged from his left ear. Then a myriad of wasps, a line of them, crawled from his nostrils, popping their wings when freed from tight confines. Herman's face grew black, yellow, and red with the insects.

"He will do the same for the flies in your skull," Karl promised. "We've paid him well. Don't fight it." He let go of Baldric's chin, and then he loosened the bandage above his ear. He did not cradle the bandage, or observe the larvae on it, or talk of washing it. Karl simply threw the cloth to the ground. It was stained fully red and brown now. "Place your hand in Werner," he said. He did not wait for Baldric to acquiesce. Rather, he took Baldric's hand and forced it into the wet matter of Werner's skull. It was a repulsive touch. Offal. Karl gripped so tightly that he nearly broke the bones in Baldric's wrist.

Baldric's head throbbed. Feeling, sensation, returned to his mouth and neck. His heart quickened. Blood oozed from his wound. The flap fell open, and the larvae crawled free. As the maggots slinked, they sprouted wings and leapt forth. Larvae flew from his face, joining the wasps on Herman's corpse, forming an odd, quivering orb. For several minutes, larvae crawled from Baldric's wound. Then he felt the worms in his throat. He opened his mouth, and the larvae crawled across his tongue and lips. Sprouting wings (he could taste the wired texture of the wings), the larvae flew from his mouth. The maggots did the same from his nostrils. Then, in the most horrid motion, the larvae squirmed from his eye sockets. There had been a thousand or more flies under his skin and within his skull.

The orb of wasp and fly took on an alchemical glow. It was the same light Baldric had seen before. It was the light in the forest. He could even see green veins where the wasps and flies merged. The light of the orb grew stronger.

"The Lost Christian," Karl said.

It was the last thing Baldric remembered hearing, yet he saw one thing more. A dark shape, that of a man's spindly body, grew beneath the light and then stepped from the crucified form of Herman. The uncanny body reached a hand towards Baldric. God was merciful then. Baldric's mind shut out the world, the stigmas in his eyes grew complete. With a shudder, he fainted.

It was in the midst of soldiers that he awoke.

"The habit of a monk," one of the men said, and he spoke German. "Benedictine."

Baldric started. He made a motion to flee, startled that he possessed the energy to do so. In fact, he felt well rested and strong, as if he had been napping. He curled his fingers, amazed that there was life in his digits now, feeling. The sense of touch had returned to him. He must've looked like a fool, rubbing his fingertips together with awe written across his face.

The man leaning over him, holding a lantern and smelling of leather and horseflesh, said, "Relax, brother. You're in safe hands." He wore a scarlet doublet with a bandolier. Soiled ruffs surrounded his wrists. A pistol and a sword were at his side.

"Where am I?" Baldric asked. His confusion, too, had cleared. He felt alive and well. The question was genuine, not a muddled refrain.

"You're in the back of a wagon now."

And healed, Baldric thought, astonished.

As the soldier said this, Baldric realized he was moving. The planks under his back jostled atop an uneven road.

The stars were bright in the sky, and it was cold. Trees, their underbelly lighted by the lantern, passed overhead. The leaves were falling now. Summer finally relinquished its grip.

"We are on our way to Ingolstadt," the soldier said. He was a young man, well bred, handsome, blond. His features were noble. A metal helmet, pinioned with once-bright feathers, lay on the planks at his side. A cache of battered swords rested, waited, against the wagon wall. "We found you in a village north of Dachau." He stopped, remembering the grisly sight. "A burned village," he added. "Are you well enough to listen? I can allow you to sleep more."

Baldric nodded. "I've slept enough. I know what you saw at the village."

The soldier shook his head. His eyes were thoughtful, drawn inward. "We believed you were dead. You had—" he motioned to the side of his head. "Just a terrible wound. God is watching out for you, though. Feel your scalp."

Baldric touched his head. It was astounding. There was no bandage. The bristle of hair met his fingertips. His ear was undamaged. There was no blood, no flap of skin, nothing grotesque, nothing out of the ordinary.

The soldier laughed. "A miracle," he said. "We need miracles in these times."

"Amen," another soldier said, a man who, until now, had been silent. He was sitting on the edge of the wagon, his booted legs hanging from the back. He looked like a boy on a hayride rather than a killer of men.

"Was there another man with me?" Baldric asked. "A large man with red hair."

"I'm afraid not. There was a man, though his face was mutilated, hanging against a tree. There was another on the ground with his head smashed in. I couldn't tell the color of his hair, but he was very small. Both men were small."

"No others?"

"Not with you. There were many villagers...."

Baldric sat up. *Karl*, he thought. The memory was vivid. He thought of the pulsing orb. The hand that had reached for him, that had apparently healed him. Blacking out had done nothing to diminish the details. He remembered everything. *What have you done, Karl? Where did you follow it?*

"I'll leave you to your thoughts, brother," the blond soldier said.

"Please don't. One of my companions is still lost in that forest. He found something beguiling there, I fear. He's following wherever it will take him."

The soldier gestured apologetically. "We haven't the time to search for lost men. There are stories," he began, "of a—"

Baldric shook his head. "An impostor," he said abruptly. "There is no Lost Christian in that forest. Although whatever it is may think that of itself. Maybe it sponges thoughts when it looks inside you."

The soldier, finding all of this enigmatic, nodded. "Perhaps," he said. He placed his lantern on a hook at the side of the wagon. The flame shook, quivering the light.

The wagon moved on through the night. A pistoleer on horseback, wearing a breastplate over a buff coat, came alongside the wagon. He made no effort to be silent. Everything about the man said that he was bringing havoc to the procession. His nervous energy was like an aura. "There's a fire burning in Ingolstadt," he said.

"Tell the men to prepare to make haste," the blond said.

The mounted soldier pushed through the ranks, shouting orders as he went. His nervous energy was contagious, and it erupted throughout the company. The sleepy procession was no more.

What have you done? Baldric thought. He asked the question of himself, and he asked the question again of Karl. He stopped short of asking the question of God, but the temptation was there. He'd allowed the thought, and now here it was again. *Feed a stray cat once, and it stays forever,* he thought. A great deal of penance awaited him.

"I heard that story as a boy," the soldier at the back of the wagon was saying. "The Lost Christian. The miller." He chuckled.

As he gathered his gear, the blond stopped and smacked at the planks. "Odd for a wasp to be out at night," he said. He stood, and then he hopped to the road. He lifted the lantern and walked alongside. He said something inaudible to the wagoner. The man nodded and turned to look at Brother Baldric.

The other soldier cracked his neck and hopped from the wagon as well. "It's the late summer. It has the wasps drunk with confusion. Remember that quivering mass of them around Dachau?"

The blond nodded. He lifted his helmet from the wagon bed and started away. "Perhaps," he said. "Stay safe, brother. I was hoping your rest would last longer."

"*Dominus vobiscum,*" Baldric said. *The Lord be with you.* He went to his knees and prayed.

The wagon fell behind as horses and men moved around it.

THE SECOND IMPOSTOR:

THE
NIGHTSHADE
GARDEN

orin Toth stared into a fireless hearth. An hour had passed since one of the servants escorted him to the library and asked him to wait. He waited, nursing a snifter of wine. Although he'd finished two glasses, he still failed to pinpoint the aroma. The wine had the quality of cut flowers. He drank, and he worried about his greyhound, Vinegar Tom. The dog, which always traveled with Toth, had gone to the stables with horses to be cleaned and fed. Despite a tendency to be contrary, Vinegar Tom hated to be alone. Toth had little choice, however. The servant made it clear the animal was not welcome inside, not until he'd had a scrub.

Presently, sunlight entered the library through four windows, two on each side of the hearth, perfectly symmetrical. Dust moved in the shafts of light. The library was a curiosity and temptation. Finer and more complete in its contents, Toth supposed, than the university in Vienna, the complex of rooms held many thousands of volumes, pressings, and relics. A cabinet of curiosities even occupied one of the corners. Books and manuscripts lined shelves that reached floor to ceiling—more material than one could digest in two lifetimes. The room was, like the floral wine, enchanting.

Toth stood, drink making him bold, and began to examine the shelves. He had traveled here to Hungary, risking a great deal in this hostile time, in order to purchase two rare volumes from the collection of Magdalen Sarkozy. A member of the Hungarian peerage, Sarkozy had an admittedly vague connection to Emperor Leopold in Austria. It was through this connection that Toth, at his university in Vienna, had learned of her unique collection. She would, he decided, have to forgive his curiosity and snooping. He stopped between two great walls of books. The arrangement presented an interesting dichotomy. Volumes of the sciences, from the *Novum Organum* of Francis Bacon to treatises on herbalism and binary numbers, were on the wall at his left. The other side of the room better suited his temper. A collection of occult works stood as a mirror image of the library of science. Handwritten manuscripts, texts that existed in a few copies scattered around the world, lined the shelves. He shuffled through the titles, exploring. The wealth it would require to compile such a collection astounded him. He lifted a manuscript, bound in a simple folio, and turned the leather cover to read the title: *The Marauder's Lantern*. Amazed, he thought, *how did you ever come by this, Madam Sarkozy?* Toth himself had saved this volume from permanent destruction (the only copy, he'd presumed at the time) a decade prior. Apparently he'd been wrong about the book's singularity. *She could lock me in, and I'd never complain*, he thought then. *I'd go mad trying to read them all. And willingly.* Every book like *The Marauder's Lantern* was the sum of a lifetime's learning. And there were hundreds like it. He knelt at another shelf of manuscripts. The first title he spied was the *Hieroglyphs of Ba'al.* He wondered if Sarkozy consulted these books, if she understood them.

The stuffed, disorganized shelves amused him. The books here were not catalogued and arranged like those on the opposite side of the room. The arrangement was a statement: the sciences were ordered, and the occult was messy. He appreciated the sentiment.

Toth lifted the *Hieroglyphs of Ba'al.* An embroidered and carefully manicured title page greeted him. Toth had spent a lifetime tracking down and deciphering magical books, and yet the *Hieroglyphs* eluded him until now. He knew of it from his days as a student. Some of his colleagues believed it legendary. He'd always assumed it would be found in Egypt, in Luxor.

A servant opened the library door. Hazy, natural light from the hall crossed the threshold. The man stood with his back to the open room, preferring the reverence of facing his master. Magdalen Sarkozy passed the servant without a word and stepped inside.

Toth replaced the *Hieroglyphs* on the shelf, as painful as it was to let the book slip from his grasp. He wondered if she'd be willing to sell this book, as well. The price, no doubt, would test the university's loyalty to him.

Sarkozy had the presence of a fine stage actor. She filled the room.

Toth stepped from the shelves and bowed. "Dorin Toth, madam."

With refined posture, Sarkozy stood there a moment with sunlight touching the hem of her antiquated dress. She matched Toth in age, being close to either side of fifty. Her natural hair had gone gray, a fact she did not conceal beneath a wig (the practice in Austria). Toth appreciated that—he, too, shunned the style, finding lilac wigs more fitting for a peacock. Without effort, Sarkozy exuded an elegance that reached inside Toth. He felt her magnetism keenly.

She smiled, but the warmth of the gesture did not reach her pale eyes. Sarkozy approached. "German?" she asked.

"If you prefer, Madam Sarkozy," Toth said. German was the language of the court in nearby Pressburg. To speak Hungarian, even in Hungary, signified a lack of education. It was a vulgar peasant tongue. In a rehearsed tone, he said, "It is my esteemed pleasure to be in your presence. Your hospitality is well known. Your wine," he said, looking away momentarily at the empty glass on the table beside his chair, "deserves to be equally known." He nearly gushed about the library's opulence then but managed to check his rambling.

Sarkozy smiled, more genuinely now, at his accent. It was an accent, with years of training, she had carefully erased. As everyone in this region had done thus far in his travels, she eyed the red scarf at Toth's neck. He wore it always. "You are of the Romani," she said. "It is bold to proclaim such a thing here." She looked back at the servant tending the door, a Roma man, and then to Toth. The gesture sank his heart.

"I am," he said.

"Dr. Dorin Toth," she said, "we have much to discuss. And you won't find your books in here. We'll talk in the open air of the gardens."

"That would be agreeable," Toth said, although he had no desire to leave the library.

"Come." Sarkozy turned on her heel and started from the room. Her servant still held the door. Toth was tempted to ask Sarkozy why she employed Roma servants. The men who had welcomed him off the boat were Roma, as well. The Romani were an oppressed people here, it was true, but they were also nomadic, passing from village to village as a mode of life. It was odd to see so many serving in sedentary roles.

As the three passed through a corridor lined with windows on one wall and hanging portraits on the opposite, Sarkozy said, "You do not have to walk in back of me, Master Dorin. Step up. Quickly now."

Toth hurried forward while the servant remained in the rear. The floor here was stone, but long carpets of Russian design muted the footfalls.

By his side now, she said, "I hope the Turks were no issue on your journey. They are everywhere nowadays. Plentiful as vermin."

"Quite nearly they were an issue," Toth admitted. "Vienna is under siege. They're as near you as Pressburg, patrolling the shores."

"God's grace has kept them from this estate," she said, and the tone suggested a joke. A strand of gray hair loosened, falling over her pale forehead. "How long will you be staying with me?" she asked.

"I need to examine the texts for authenticity," he said. "That may take time."

She smiled. "I hope you don't rush."

"Madam, have you consulted these texts? Or any like them in your library?"

"I've made an effort to understand them," Sarkozy said. She let it go at that. "I read your treatise on grimoires. It was in the *Philosophical Transactions*, no?"

She possessed, he'd noticed, a collection of the journal in her library, and it was located properly on the scientific side of the room. "I was certain it appeared in that journal for amusement," he said. With embarrassment, he recalled the commentary that had accompanied the piece.

After a turn through another long, open hallway, twin doors opened onto the first of the gardens. The aroma of earth and sweet decay washed over Toth. The garden was sumptuous and overgrown, having obliterated lines of design. Flowers from the Americas and Mediterranean clustered with flora of the Carpathians. Sarkozy gestured towards a mass of plants she had been cultivating. She had, of late, been collecting species endemic to Russia as a hobby. She very much admired Tsar Peter, she said. She then showed a rare spleenwort in the shade, but complained at her inability to keep the fern alive. "It prefers higher air," she commented.

Sarkozy led the way through a hedge tunnel, where sunlight broke through the leaves in pieces. A family of gray and white cats, tired of the heat, lounged inside. The animals did not seem perturbed about the stranger who stepped over them. A stone fence began on the other side of the long arbor. The fence was squat and weathered dark, with moss growing thickly over the stone. Laurel grew along the top of the fence, making a poisonous barrier of cyanide. The fence was as old as the mansion—several hundred years, Toth assumed.

With pride, Sarkozy warned, "Here is the poison garden. Don't touch the plants, Master Dorin. All of them have the ability to harm." She pushed the wrought-iron gate inward. The poison garden was small in comparison to the expansive trees shadowing it, and it was clean and ordered in comparison to the surrounding gardens. Inside the rectangular enclosure stretched a floor with rock cut into tiles of various shapes. A stone table with two wooden chairs stood at the center. Beds of purple and green plants, with leaves architecturally designed and often cupping bright flowers, lined the edge and buttressed the fence. There was violet nightshade, seven-leaved saptaparna, angel's trumpet, pungent henbane, wolfsbane, mandrake, and other plants Sarkozy didn't name. The poison garden was an eccentric and lethal showpiece.

"Impressive," he told Sarkozy, but for the moment he worried about the wine he drank so freely.

The servant arranged the seats, keeping his eyes down. Once Sarkozy and Toth were seated, the young man stepped through the gate and left the garden.

Sarkozy looked around. "The birds and insects stay clear of this space," she said. "Everything does." She pointed at a dry mess of stalks. "Even the rain, it seems. It is the safest place on the grounds. My favorite."

"Are there villages on your lands?" Toth asked. He was curious as to the extent of the Sarkozy family holdings. Hungarian nobles didn't hold titles like Duchess or Countess, so it was unapparent whether their nobility was high or low. Wealth, however, spoke.

"Two villages. Domhaza and Ferenc. Domhaza is ten leagues distant, perhaps. With the Turks about it's a great deal of responsibility. Leopold's war has been a drain. The villagers need constant protection. Turks are as good as pirates. Sometimes they travel the river in small bands. It's not always an army one has to watch for."

"Raiders," Toth agreed. "I saw no Turks on the river near. Truth be told, I found that odd. By the look of your home, they've never been near."

The servant returned with a tray holding two glasses and a decanter of wine. He arranged the glasses and poured the drinks. Then he was gone again. Sunlight glinted off the polished tray.

Toth sipped. He recognized the bouquet now. The aroma matched that of the garden.

Sarkozy noticed his sudden pallor. "Don't trouble yourself about the ingredients," she said, suppressing a grin. "This wine won't harm you." Delicately, she took a drink from her glass. "It does wonders for the complexion, though."

Toth touched his glass but refrained from another sip. "How do you manage to keep the Turks distant?" he asked. "I noticed no watchman in the tower."

Sarkozy smiled. "There are watchmen about." After a tick of silence, she said, "Tell me about the books you're buying, Dr. Toth. What will you do with them? Speak on your subject, sir. I love to hear it."

From the edge of the gardens, Toth could see Magdalen Sarkozy standing in front of a second story window, watching the river. The Sarkozy estate, with the sun now behind it, was strangely beautiful. For a moment, he could only stand and admire. Wrapped by the garden and shadowed by trees, the venerable mansion stood in three sections: the foremost and largest, intricate as lace, at the center with a smaller wing flanking each side. Although by no means a castle, the home breathed old wealth. It was imposing and built with cut stone. The windows comprised a variety of shapes: a balance of quarter arches, pentagons, and cathedral arches. The roofing was iron colored slate, interrupted by decorative chimneys and a belvedere with glass windows at the center. A fenced balcony jutted from the belvedere, high enough to watch the Danube for a mile in each direction. No watchman occupied the perch.

The grandness of the sight moved Toth, partially because it was a fading grandness. He looked for Sarkozy in the window again, but she had gone. Toth dismissed the spell of his thoughts. He needed to check on Vinegar Tom. The greyhound would be terribly anxious.

Where the gardens ended, a grassy knoll began. Toth turned from the home and started up a narrow footpath that led to the stables. Rather than a barn, the stables were erected in a rectangular line of stalls, each stall with a gate and awning. Pastel blue, chipping into petals, covered the planks. The stalls had been quiet, but as Toth stepped from the footpath and onto crushed stone, Vinegar Tom's sharp face popped up from behind one of the doors. He stood at his full height, with his paws and thin snout over the edge of the door. He barked with a mix of panic and joy. His barking stirred the horses.

Toth unlatched the gate and, as soon as there was a crack of freedom, Tom bounded forth. The dog forgot his usual sourness as he circled Toth breathlessly, his tongue lolling and ears pricked. "Now, now," Toth said. He scratched Vinegar Tom's neck and patted his prominent ribs. His coat was still damp. The dog had been, as promised, scrubbed clean. "Now, now," he said. Tom, a product of Kent, preferred his master to speak English, and this Toth did.

The serene moment—with the sun at his back and the sounds of the river, of Tom's panting, of the breeze and birds—shattered when Tom stiffened and cut loose with a frantic bark. Toth first thought one of the servants had approached, yet, when he turned to see, no one stood on the path. Rather, the dog leapt towards a stand of trees behind the stables. Toth's second thought was that a cat stole the dog's attention. Tom could be cruel with small animals, and that wasn't the impression Toth wanted to make, not with Sarkozy or one of her servants looking on.

Sprinting around the side of the stables, Toth entered a grove of evergreens. Bundles of mistletoe pocked the branches, and dead needles blanketed the earth. The canopy was thick enough to keep the ground steeped in shadow. Tom, as if his mother had bitten his nape, now stood rigid and silent. Toth slowed when he saw the dog's changed manner. A sense of dread crept forward in his mind. His third thought was that a snake from the river had appeared. A snake, though, would not leave the dog cowed. Tom would posture and make a show even as he inched away.

He joined Tom and looked down at the bed of needles. Indeed, a small calico cat stood there, but she, too, was rigid with fear. The cat and dog, in fact, stared at the same object on the ground. A large river rat stood cornered against the trunk of one of the pines. The rodent was charcoal gray and rivaled the cat in girth. Sap matted its coat. Its eyes were little black points.

A harbinger of plague, Toth thought jokingly. *Who wouldn't be frightened?* Just as he knelt and pinched a stone from the ground to break the standoff, his lightness drained away. The rat, he saw then, had the well-articulated hands and digits of a human infant. The thing was an abomination, a chimera. The rodent stood palms downward, and the familiar lines of knuckles and nails protruded. The skin had the purple, mottled shade of a newborn. In horror, Toth grew still. As he watched, the fur on the arm of the rat receded, revealing another patch of mottled flesh below.

Toth unsheathed a dagger from his belt. At the glint of metal, as if the thing recognized the threat, the rat scuttled quickly into the shadows of the grove.

"Kill it," Toth ordered Vinegar Tom. The greyhound's chest expanded. As the calico made her escape towards the stables, Toth and his dog chased the rat. The grove led into a thicket of undergrowth, filled with thorns and tall weeds. The bramble led downward to the river with no discernible path to interrupt it. It was a barrier the rat navigated, hugging the ground, but it halted Toth and his dog. The animal trembled. Toth understood the feeling.

He felt the shaking in his own hand acutely as he tried to put away the dagger. He had to use both hands to accomplish the task.

Toth watched the riverbank for any sign of the rat. Audaciously, the thing did not remain hidden in the undergrowth. It moved into the mud of the shore, scampering towards the water. The rat looked, from this distance, to have grown. Less fur and more flesh covered its arms. The rat walked directly into the lapping tide, keeping its hands against the ground rather than swimming. It walked until submerged. The long tail was the last to sink below.

Toth watched the water, waiting for the rodent to pop up and float away, yet it never did. After several minutes, he and Tom pushed through the final barrier of thorns. Upon the shore, he looked at the prints in the mud, which were a mix of rat claws and human hands. It was then that a man emerged on the opposite shore. The man walked directly from the water, as if he had crossed the vast expanse of the Danube by walking along the floor. Although he was too distant to make out features, the man wore no clothing and had the dark skin of the Romani. He walked into the opposing forest.

A harbinger indeed, Toth thought, horrified and astonished.

Through the open window, rain against the trees and gardens made a pleasant, calming sound. This was right—the world was correct with nothing askew. Toth folded his arms on the sill and tried to assure himself. The rat wasn't imagination. Tom, too, had seen it. He cupped his face and tried to gather himself. Save for a candle on a side table, his room had grown dark. Suddenly, the touch of a cold nose against his arm startled him. He turned to find Vinegar Tom, miserable for want of attention, resting his head against his master's leg. The dog murmured. He was hungry and disturbed.

Toth bent and kissed the dog's forehead. "You're a brave old codger," he told the greyhound. "Braver than me. You went after it, didn't you?"

The dog shivered when a drop of rain reached him.

At least you're not out with the horses, Toth thought gratefully. *Or the rat.* Once Toth had requested it, Sarkozy allowed the animal limited access to her home. Tom was permitted in the bedroom and corridor, but he was forbidden to roam free.

Toth lowered the window and stepped away. He used the burning wick to light three more candles around the room. Darkness receded, quivering at the edge. The room was more an apartment than bedroom. A massive fireplace dominated one of the walls, while a four-poster bed with heavy curtains dominated another. Two windows looked out over the gardens and down to the river. This was only one of the rooms within the bedroom. At one point in the mansion's past, this had been private living quarters in a multi-generational household. It felt odd to imagine the estate filled with life. It was impossible to imagine the ruckus of children here.

Toth started when a knock came at the door. It was a quick, polite rapping. Tom ridged his back. *We've both had nerves,* Toth thought. He crossed a Russian carpet and opened the door. To his chagrin, a servant stood there, one of the Romani. Toth had hoped for Sarkozy.

In Hungarian, the man said, "I apologize for the disturbance, Master Toth."

"Come inside," Toth said.

The servant obeyed. "Madam Sarkozy requests your presence, sir."

It was on his mind, and it bothered him, so he asked, "Why are all the servants here of the Romani? That's odd, isn't it?"

The servant, watching Vinegar Tom with unease, nodded.

"Don't mind the dog. He's harmless," Toth said.

"Yes, sir," the servant said, but his eyes said otherwise. The dog frightened him.

"Why do you stay here?" Toth persisted.

"Madam treats us fairly, sir."

"I don't doubt it, but it's against your nature. I've never seen so many Romani anchored to one household."

Again the servant nodded. A look of shame spread on his face. Whatever he wanted to say, he swallowed. He lowered his eyes. "Madam Sarkozy is waiting, sir. Your animal will dine in this room."

Without another word the man shut Tom inside and led Toth through the corridor and down a staircase wrought with tulips. The Romani were a loyal people. In the young man's mind, he had already betrayed Sarkozy by speaking to the guest. The servant walked through a set of twin doors and entered the east wing of the estate. A tapestry depicting a battle between Vlad Dracula and the Turks hung above the doorway.

Sarkozy stood in the softly lighted hall, waiting. She dismissed the servant and beckoned Toth. "Did you find the books satisfactory?" she asked.

Toth shook his head. "I haven't looked over them," he admitted. "I was distracted." He hadn't, in fact, even taken them from their sheathing.

"Fatigue from your journey, no doubt. Would you like to dine in the garden?" she asked.

"I'm afraid it's raining, madam," Toth said, puzzled.

Sarkozy laughed a little. "Maybe it isn't fatigue. Maybe you're feverish, Master Dorin. There's no rain."

I heard it and felt it, Toth thought, wondering at what seemed a trivial disagreement.

Sarkozy frowned. "Are you ill, sir?"

It was the one moment he considered confessing what he witnessed by the stables, but doubt kept him silent. His doubt grew stronger as he faced Sarkozy. *What if it were not raining?* he thought. *What would that mean? I saw that, too. And Tom—he shivered at it. Perhaps,* he thought then, *I am ill.* He hadn't considered this. The reality settled on him, and he disliked it. "Just fatigued," he said finally.

"Come then. Dinner is prepared."

Once outside, a clear night sky proved Sarkozy correct. By the appearance of the pathway and surrounding leaves, there had been no rain in quite some time. It was dreamlike, and Toth wondered again about the wine.

The table in Sarkozy's poison garden held four silver trays. The meal was delicate and vegetarian. The ubiquitous floral wine was present. Four servants, all of whom were elderly Roma women with red scarves at their necks, held candelabra at the corners of the garden. They said nothing and stood very still. Only occasionally did their lights tremble.

Across the table, Sarkozy asked, "Where is your rain, Master Dorin?"

He feigned a laugh. "Perhaps I was sleeping," he said, but inside he felt sick.

As Toth's doubt increased, Sarkozy seemed the opposite: she grew bolder, more confident. The transfer was vampiric. "Scholars don't fall asleep at books," she teased. "Only us normal folk do such things."

For a reason he couldn't fathom, he sipped the wine. He was compelled. There was something enchanting about the feeling that followed the taste. One could grow dependent on such a thing. He sipped again and felt calmer. Then, with sincerity, Toth asked, "How did you ever amass such a library?"

"I don't deserve sole credit for that," Sarkozy said. "My grandfather and father and my brother, before he passed, procured many of those books. I've added more than a few. Poison interests me. And the Hermetic books. And the Romani," she added, "are of great interest to me."

"Why is that?"

She played with her glass as she watched Toth. "Would you really like to know?"

"I would."

"I find your people transcendent. 'Liminal' is the proper word for a scholar like you. Take a German, say. If he's summer, then the Romani are spring. If he's winter then you're autumn. He is a thing, and you're between things. Romani can cross that threshold with or without university. All of these servants know vulgar magic, folk magic. Every one of them. I'm inclined to think it's in your blood."

Toth didn't know the extent to which he agreed, but he said, "It's a way of seeing the world. Your villagers would call that witchcraft."

"Perhaps," she said, "they would. You were born among the Romani? You traveled with them?"

Toth nodded. "Then my father sent me to Vienna."

"To escape what?"

Toth looked at one of the old servants. Their eyes did not meet. "To escape that," he said. "Servitude."

"And it was there you learned higher magic. Did you lose the lower sort? Do the books obscure that ability or is it still there? You must tell me. It fascinates me."

"I have to admit you fascinate me," Toth said. He felt her magnetism. Busy hands betrayed his nerves. Sinfully, his face flushed.

She waited.

"It's always there," he said.

Just then a young man came running into the garden. He was breathless. He looked at Toth and then Sarkozy, as if asking permission to speak freely. "Go on," Sarkozy ordered in Hungarian. "What is it?"

"A Turkish commander and his inferior," the servant said. "They were traveling the river."

Toth went cold.

"Alone?" Sarkozy asked. "Where are they now?"

"They've been subdued, madam. They're waiting in the cottage."

"They've what?" Toth asked.

Sarkozy turned to him. "You wondered at the absence of Turks," she said. "Shall I show you how it's accomplished? Would you like to see a watchman?"

Toth braced himself and nodded.

Sarkozy led Toth towards the stables on the opposite side of the estate. Oddly, once beyond the garden, it appeared as though it *had* been raining that night. The grass was slick and the trees oily in the moonlight. A thin fog crept in from the river. Toth said nothing of the paradox. Dread of the Turks kept him silent. He looked above as they passed beneath his bedroom window. Vinegar Tom had his paws on the sill, looking downward, vigilant as Toth passed. *Now you have a proper watchman,* Toth thought. A part of him wished he had Tom near for protection. *At least you're safe, old friend,* he thought.

The cottage, a mirror image of those found in Carpathian villages, stood in rear of the horse stalls. Strangely, Toth hadn't noticed the structure earlier that day. It was not something one would miss. He would swear that there had been nothing except the pine grove here. Now the cottage stood prominently where trees had been before. Even the trees surrounding the cottage had changed from pine to ash. *Everything here is in a state of flux,* he realized, and Sarkozy's word, liminal, surfaced again. He half expected to close his eyes and open them to daylight, but when he did this the night remained. The cottage was colorful and pale with vines of pink leaves painted on the shutters. The roof was thatch. In front of the cottage, rendering it a church of sorts, stood a Greek cross wrapped in beads. The ash grove around the cottage was silent. The horses in their stalls were silent.

A light burned inside the cottage. The door stood ajar.

Sarkozy nodded to the servant, a knowing gesture, and the young man walked past the building and entered the bramble. He slipped into the darkness as if walking into water. A few delicate snaps from his footfalls, and then Toth and Sarkozy were alone.

"A beautiful cottage," she said. "The beauty of *volksmusik.*"

"They're inside?" Toth asked, anxious to have the confrontation over and done with.

"Like the beauty of *volkshexen*," Sarkozy continued. She gestured to the shadow, where the Roma had gone. She turned her eyes to Toth. "*Er kann hexen*," she said. *He knows magic.*

Toth's dread intensified. The atmosphere froze the thoughts in his mind. Thinking clearly was impossible. He'd seen what Turks had done to villages like Maria Enzersdorf. That carnage unfolded without inviting their wrath.

Sarkozy appeared untroubled. Calm and confident, and with an undercurrent of pleasure, she looked with pity at Toth's shaking hands. "The books you search for, Dorin. What is it that you look for inside them?"

His mouth was parched. "Knowledge," he managed to say.

"Knowledge of what?" Sarkozy moved a strand of gray from her face. Her face was close to his, so that Toth felt her warmth.

"The occult," he said.

"Call it what it is. Do you look for magic?"

Toth nodded.

"Higher magic. You look for what is already inside you." She touched his face. "Let me show you." She stepped inside the cottage and beckoned him to follow.

This he did.

Two wax candles, suspended in sockets against the front wall, lit the interior. Four straw mats lay against packed dirt. Two of the mats were empty, and two held the docile, languid bodies of Turkish soldiers. The men were tied in place, immobile, but still they lived. A device that looked like something to aid in forcing medicine down animal gullets kept their lips parted and mouths wide. The Turks were stripped to undergarments, and their ornate uniforms lay in piles on the floor, but still the men were identifiable by their dark beards and the rings of carnelian and amethyst on their hands. With leaden eyes, the soldiers watched Magdalen Sarkozy and Dorin Toth. The men were, despite initial appearance, aware. Terror lay beneath the paralyzed muscles of their faces. Unintelligible noises, efforts to speak, gargled from their throats.

"Madam," Toth started, as if in protest, but Sarkozy put her hand on his arm, and he stopped.

"Do not say something untrue. You know what needs to be done. Watchmen," she reminded. Sarkozy said this in accented Hungarian rather than German. The gesture was the lowering of a mask. Her hand ran to his, and she gripped before releasing him.

In one of the shadowed corners of the cottage, the pelting of dirt, a subtle noise like that of broadcasted seeds, arrested the room. Weakly, the Turks tried to rise from their mats. Straw crunched and ropes groaned. Toth watched the dark corner. His pulse throbbed. Something tunneled beneath the packed floor.

For a moment, the cottage was still except for the Turks' labored breathing. Then there was a scuttling of claws against dirt. In the shadow Toth saw the form of a rat—the same rat, he supposed, that he'd seen previously in the grove. The rodent moved to the nearest mat. The air around the rat's spine quivered, like air around a flame. The rat opened its mouth impossibly wide, unhinging its jaw like a snake, and then the rodent's chest heaved. A busy tongue touched yellow teeth. Again the rat heaved, as if dislodging something from deep in its gut.

Toth started to look away, but Sarkozy urged his attention. He watched.

Onto the floor, the rat vomited the peculiar shape of a toad. Slick with bile, the toad hopped towards the mat. Warts studded its brown skin. The Turk was too drugged to fight, but his leg twitched in protest. The rat, unfazed, heaved and vomited a second toad. This toad was smaller and less pocked by warts. It, too, moved to the mat. Free of the burden, the rat shook itself like a wet dog and began crawling up the side of the Turk, hooking its back claws as a grip. Cloth tore under the thing's considerable weight.

Once on the chest of the soldier, the rat altered its shape, the lines of its body blurring. The fur on its right arm receded, revealing mottled flesh. The front claws morphed into the shape of human hands. The Turk could not resist. To the man's horror, the rat unhinged its jaw and approached his face. The rodent heaved. A small toad disgorged from its throat and fell against soldier's beard. The rat maneuvered until its teeth lay against the man's lips. Then it took another step, moving its head into his mouth. The rat heaved rapidly, its back muscles clinching and arching, its coarse fur splitting and revealing purplish skin. Small hands gripped the man's chest. The rat vomited living toads down the Turk's throat and into his stomach.

"You would kill them this way?" Toth asked.

Sarkozy said, "Not at all. They will live and return to their men, but altered. They'll think and speak from their stomach now."

"What will they do when they return to their men?"

Sarkozy offered a weary grin. "They will do what needs to be done."

"And if they return here? What then?"

"They've never returned here," Sarkozy said.

And so it was. That very night the Turks returned on the river to their men.

The coal black current lapped against the edge of the flatboat. Morning fog lay over the river, shrouding the shores. The boatmen, ancient Barna at the fore and his son János at the aft, navigated the Danube with deft skill. Each man wielded a pole, guiding the vessel. Once the Sarkozy estate was out of sight, the river entered a forest, and the fog deepened. Mistletoe, once abundant along the shores, disappeared from the trees.

Toth stood on the planks towards the center of the boat, protecting the satchel of three manuscripts he'd purchased. He listened to the water, and more than a sleepless night weighed on his mind. He stared at the fog and wondered at an exchange he'd had with Sarkozy before departing. She'd escorted him to the poison garden once more that night, this time without servants or light, and proffered a vial of nightshade.

If it's too much, she'd said, meaning the abomination of the rat and the personal ritual Toth had undergone by witnessing it, *this is the surest way out.*

He'd taken the vial but had no intention of using the poison. He felt altered by the experience. *I've lived to see such things,* he'd said. Then, with hope, *What is the name of the servant? May I speak to him?*

Magdalen Sarkozy would not reveal his name.

Toth left with the vial. He held it now, with the manuscripts, in his satchel.

Vinegar Tom, on his stomach due to a lack of sea legs, crawled forward and nudged his boot. Drawn from the trance, Toth knelt and scratched the dog's ears. Tom pouted. The greyhound wanted desperately to be home again. He was sick of traveling. "Soon," Toth comforted. "Soon, old friend."

"There's another one," Barna shouted from the front of the boat. "Get to the right of it."

With a heave that tested the sturdy forearms of the boatmen, the vessel lurched to the right.

"Clear?" János asked.

"That oughta do it," Barna said. "Steady now." After a moment of silence, the old man added, "Four of 'em this morning. I don't like it a bit."

János agreed. He muttered a Hungarian couplet, the type of prayer inscribed above doorways in country villages. He crossed his heart at the finish of the words.

Toth patted Vinegar Tom and stood. Feeling old in the knees, he got free of the canvas tarpaulin and joined Barna.

A caparison, dark as the water, floated near the edge of the boat. It was the decorative cape worn by horses in the Turkish cavalry. A hem with gilded threading dragged against the planks as it passed.

"Four?" Toth asked.

Barna, a mercurial man, looked at Toth and then back at the caparison. "I'm tempted to snatch it up," the boatman said. "It would fetch a good price, but what would it mean to get caught with such a thing?" He laughed then and shrugged.

Toth nodded. To be caught with a caparison would mean enslavement. It was better to let the money drown.

Barna said, "No, not four of those. Four of those, I meant." He pointed through the swirling fog. Towards the center of the river floated the remains of a horse. The hulking corpse bobbed with the waves, and a disfigured snout jutted upward like the joint of a sawyer. The teeth were exposed. The animal was rigid.

"The fourth horseman," Barna joked. He laughed and then turned sour again.

"It may well be," Toth said. He watched as the horse fell behind, outdistanced by the speedier boat. The wake sent the snout below, and then a leg and hoof popped from the water.

Barna looked ahead, straining to see. After a moment, he said, "The way I heard it, a Turk commander went mad and killed his men not far from here last night. That's the word. Seeing all these horses I'm inclined to believe it."

Toth felt a chill. "You should believe it," he said.

Barna nodded, but his mind was in a different place. "Mother mountain has a way of dealing with Turks. *The Children of Mars have no place here.*" He was quoting something, although Toth knew not what.

Toth retreated from the boatman and joined Vinegar Tom. *Believe it if you're able.* He thought about the vial of nightshade in his satchel. Not everyone could believe such a thing. Not every mind would accept it. He felt Sarkozy's magnetism now, even from this distance, and it came upon him how painful it had been to leave her estate. It had been she who insisted. The decision was not his. He wondered if he would have ever left under his own power.

As the river carved its path through the forest, the fog started to lift. The sun emerged, and the tarpaulin's shelter became more agreeable. He took a seat beside Tom.

Again the greyhound pouted. "Now, now," Toth said. "We'll be home soon enough." Looking back once more to the distant horse, he added, "We're safe." He thanked Sarkozy. The boat drifted towards the twin cities of Buda and Pest.

THE THIRD IMPOSTOR:

THE
BRINE
and BONE
ALCHEMY

The Carib moved farther out to sea. He looked back for assurance, but the island and its people were nothing more than shapes. A deep uncertainty passed through him. The raft lifted and fell, saltwater gurgling through crude planks and washing over the sides. The sun was hard against the water, almost blinding, and the sea was warm. Frigatebirds swirled in the distance, calling out, looking for shoals.

When the Carib could no longer see the bottom of the ocean, he began uncoiling the rope. Although his hands trembled, a persistent memory of the Carib's grandmother, a sage woman, kept him balanced. She was always with him, in the back of his thoughts, the selfless matriarch, but he never needed her more than he did now. At one time the ocean had been her cauldron. She'd manipulated the water and things therein from her shore. She'd stirred entities deeper even than Lonu, who was one of the Carib protectors. She'd peered into the caverns that opened in chasms below the water, and she'd worshipped there, just as the Carib would do. If she could accomplish all of that, then he could surely do this.

When doubt still gnawed at him, he relied on anger. He thought of the great ship, the men, their skin the color of the dead, wearing metal helmets and wielding metal blades. He thought of the enormous sails on their ships. He'd never seen anything so large.

He grew sick.

The Carib lowered the weighted end of the rope into the water. His hands dipped into the soupy brine. The rope went down, the stone at the end twirling like a toy, as he fed the coil into the sea. Satisfied with the depth, he tied the other end of the rope around his right ankle. His pulse quickened. Then, closing his eyes, he began the refrain. He spoke to Lonu as his grandmother had taught him.

Something tugged the rope from below.

The Carib placed his legs in the water. The raft tilted to one side, lifting.

He had to look. Ten feet below the surface, he saw the whip of a long tail. He knew the tail from stories his grandmother told of Lonu. The entity was closer to man than the higher pantheon. He was not merely spirit—he could be found in the physical world. One could see him. The Carib eased from the raft and into the water. The raft fell with a splash, and then it floated away. Deep below the surface, a massive jaw unhinged. The Carib kept at the refrain, even as saltwater slapped at his mouth. Despair and terror overwhelmed him. Then a force like an undercurrent grabbed the Carib, one violent heave, and he went under.

The gray, flaking stone could sear the most sand-hardened foot. At midday, the ledge grew hot as a torch. Clarion and Hugo, shrouded by a stand of palms, marveled at the heat—it had pressure like darkness, a weight that encased. The crystal sea, which spread to the horizon beneath the high perch, did not boil here as Ptolemy predicted. With the way the sun laid on the water, though, it was a wonder it didn't.

Clarion wrapped his feet in two large palm leaves, his boots having long since rotted to sinew. After Hugo did the same, the men scuttled like insects chased from the shade. Even through the leaves, the stone felt like the surface of a boiling pot.

The Carib's skull, which waited at the edge of the precipice, was almost sun-bleached, with bone the color of fatty milk. Denys had cleaned the skull meticulously, as though it were a souvenir to be gilded. He'd dulled his communion dagger by scraping the eye sockets and cleaning out the brain. He would fashion a cup from the skull when he returned to France, he claimed. Set aright on jawbones, the back of the cranium faced Clarion and Hugo, while the empty eyes looked over the sea. Harmless yellow teeth filled the broken-jawed mouth. The watchman, Denys called it. Clarion could no longer envision the young man who once housed the bones, although he'd known the heathen creature alive. He'd felt the grit of the boy's blood. He'd cut into his living heart.

Hugo marched to the edge of the outcropping, glanced down at his mates thirty feet below in the white sand, and then lifted the Carib from its perch. He whispered at the skull, and then he looked at Clarion. A child remained in his eyes, but only partially now.

Ass, Clarion thought, but said nothing. Something was eating at him today, something rising. He'd awakened with a scowl. He nodded, and then he looked out over the sparkling water.

Sunlight, even after a minute, scorched his leathered shoulders. If one endured the sun, it would make a man delirious, cook his brain. He had only to look at Denys for proof. The old man, his white beard grown to preposterous length, once had a religious experience when he stood too long in the sun. Denys had witnessed the Carib, although long dead by that juncture, standing on the stone ledge above the beach, fondling his disembodied skull, directing a passing ship towards the destruction of a ridge.

Pitiful man, Clarion thought. Denys had deteriorated so much that even his wife wouldn't know him now. Denys had lost something human.

"I feel today is the day," Hugo said. He cradled the skull against his bare chest. He ran his thumb along the prominent sutures. No one had dared be so gentle with the Carib when alive. Like all Caribs, the chiseled teeth in the skull had tasted the flesh of man. *Bastard heathens*, Clarion thought, remembering other encounters.

"Today," Hugo repeated, searching the horizon.

Today would be seven weeks too late, but Clarion would take it. He couldn't quite imagine what emotions would pass through his mind if the masts of the *Galion de Guise* appeared on the horizon. It would be pleasure like he'd never known. He'd never wanted a thing so much in his life. That was the true reason for traveling along the burning rock everyday: to look at the far edge of the ocean, to see if sails stood out against the blue sky. Consulting the watchman was a game of boredom, calloused but meant in jest.

The four Frenchmen were the only watchmen here, guardians of Louis and Richelieu's far-flung claim, armed with rusted muskets and blades lest the Spanish chance by. The day of estimated arrival for the *Galion de Guise* had come and gone. For the seven weeks beyond that night of worry and disappointment, despite day after day of praying and watching, the sea had been empty of all vessels. Only the occasional storm moved across the water. Not even the Caribs had visited to inquire about their lost companion.

In Clarion's heart, he wondered if the ship ever made it back to France. It sailed unaccompanied, after all. All would it take was an ill-timed storm. He remembered standing on the beach, watching as the tip of the final mast disappeared on the horizon. It was a hobgoblin of a thought: the crew, the only white men who knew about this island, lost at sea before telling another soul of the brethren they had left behind. He tried not to think about this, then or now.

Hugo placed the Carib on the ground again. He danced a little to keep his feet from burning. "Before God," he said, "they promised us."

Clarion grumbled. "They told us what we wanted to hear," he said. He felt cruel, but, to Hugo's despair, he went on. He was like his father then, lacking only the hard breath of a drunkard. "What else does one say to dying men? He tells them about Heaven."

Bruised, Hugo said, "I won't die here." He let the statement stand alone for a bit, let himself approach belief in it, then added, "I never got to marry. I never had children."

Clarion, himself a widower, said, "Marry old Denys. I imagine he could be convinced of anything now. I'm sure his wife already buried him." That was a fear in all their minds—that loved ones had moved on. *Why are you voicing such things?* he thought.

Hugo frowned. He liked Denys. He worried for the old man's fragile mind.

Clarion shrugged. *This is the one too many,* he thought, realizing why he'd awakened with such rage. *I didn't plan on dying here yesterday, but I do today. There's always a point like that, a hinge to turn on, and I've turned the corner.* Despair washed over him. He looked away from the sea towards the rising jungle at his back. The smell of rotting vegetation competed with the salt of the ocean. *I could retreat into the jungle,* he thought. Many things in the green inferno kill men quickly.

"None of us will die here now," Hugo said, his voice rising. "God be praised. Turn and look, Clarion. See it?" He jumped up and down until the palm leaves shook from his feet.

Cynically, Clarion looked over the water. Through the haze of white heat, he spotted a dark shape on the sea, miniscule at this distance. He studied it. In awe, he said, "That's not a ship."

"But it is a boat," Hugo said. "The ship could be near."

"Or the Spanish could be near. Or the Caribs." *Or even the English*, he thought, and imagined the sorry sight of four bedraggled Frenchmen with muskets and swords defending this dot of land. Clarion rushed to the edge of the cliff. He shaded his eyes from the sun.

"A boat!" Hugo shouted to Denys and Perrault, who stood near the hut on the beach. "A boat, praise God!"

The tide carried in something, be it boat or …. Realization struck Clarion. The image became clearer. He put his hand out, as if the gesture would calm Hugo, a delirious fool dancing with the skull of a dead man in his grip.

"A boat," he was singing. "A boat, a boat."

"Stop!" Clarion demanded.

Merry, Hugo asked, "Want a go with my partner?" He offered the skull.

"It isn't a boat."

"Codswallop," Hugo said, but he was soberer when he returned to the edge. With a smile creasing the patchy beard on his face, he looked hard. He shaded his eyes. He studied the shape. "How do you mean?"

"See how it moves?" Clarion asked. "With the whim of the tide. And there are only two men on it. They aren't rowing."

Hugo choked. With his fingers in the eye sockets, he let the skull dangle, a marionette gesture. "It's a raft," he said, in the deflated tone of a man conversing with Death.

Clarion sprinted along the ropey jungle trail, which descended into a sopping quagmire before hooking towards the beach. As he carefully navigated the morass of the basin, the jungle came alive around him, meeting his intrusion with bleats, squawks, and the dry swish of finger-like palms. Insects moved in clouds here—he had to press through them like fog. The only defense was motion. Leaving Hugo behind on the trail, Clarion ran through the gloom. Sunlight lanced the canopy above. The air smelled like compost. Soon he was in the hot sand, the salted air, with the ocean opening before him. A film of sweat, pricked by a breeze from the water, covered his body. His mind was still on fire. Above all, he feared the raft transported Caribs, traveling like a Trojan horse to avenge their fallen companion. It was only a matter of time until the natives came in a wave of invasion. He imagined the bay as a forest of canoes. The cannibals, with chiseled teeth, hostile.

Old Denys and Perrault, caught between fear and elation, met Clarion at the mouth of the trail. Perrault was the youngest of the men, a companion of Hugo's during their youth in Aquitaine, and he looked past Clarion for his friend. He had always given cool reception to his superior officer.

"What is it?" Denys asked. He was an old hand at this, having sailed to the Saint Lawrence River in his youth with Champlain. His was a world of jumping to the sword, a jarring existence, and he simply stood in the tide of things and allowed friction to move him, not unlike the approaching raft. Denys had spent three quarters of his life at sea, and now here he was, half-demented, holding a sword in his gnarled grip like a corsair. He had stuck the first blade in the Carib youth—and he'd done so as easy as breathing.

The raft was close enough now to spy from the beach. It lifted and fell with the waves. The figures atop the craft remained motionless, sitting, keeping balance with their palms planted, making no effort to hide from the sun. The tide pulled them in. The raft neared a shoal, upon the spine of which a colony of frigatebirds protested. Soon the black-feathered, long-winged birds filled the sky. Their red pouches swelled and glistened. The men on the raft had no reaction to this flurry of activity. They started to move, however, dipping their hands in the water to propel the craft over the bar.

Clarion pushed past Denys without answer. He bade the old man to turn around and look, to stifle his questions. He took the sword offered by Perrault. It felt odd holding the blade like a menace—the swords had been used for cutting vines and fish bellies for so long. To Clarion's relief, as he neared the water, he saw that the two men aboard the raft were not natives. Rather, these were white men, blistered and nearly dead from the sun. Denys, Perrault, and Hugo joined Clarion. The water, with a fringe of foam, lapped at their feet. The raft came nearer. The young men aboard were emaciated, skeletal at the limbs. Although they made no greeting, their eyes moved.

Jesus, no, Clarion thought. A touch of panic moved his heart, closed his throat. He recognized these men. He did not know their names, but he knew their faces. They were grunts from the *Galion de Guise.* Their presence here, in this condition, could mean one thing only.

Perrault and Hugo planted their blades in the sand and stepped into the water. No one spoke. The men on the

122

raft did not object as Perrault and Hugo pushed the craft onto the shore. One of the men let his hand trawl.

Denys knew, and he broke the heavy silence. "What happened?" he asked. He let his blade drop. "What happened to the ship?"

One of the men shook his head but said nothing. The other stared forward, blankly. His mind was gone. He looked as though he heard nothing, knew nothing, thought nothing.

"What of the crew?" Denys asked.

Perrault and Hugo lifted the staring man from the raft. Clarion and Denys lifted the other, who was light as a child.

Hugo, the optimist, remarked, "This raft didn't come from the *Galion de Guise*. It looks as though it were pieced together from driftwood."

"It's fastened in the manner of Caribs," Denys agreed.

Indeed, it was. An odd but true observation.

"In what Hell would anyone fashion a raft from driftwood?" Perrault asked.

"These men need water, food, and shade," Clarion interjected. "Put questions to them later. I can carry this one myself. Denys, gather some fruit. Perrault, accompany him. Hugo, come with me, and bring the other."

The men did as they were ordered. Each needed to gather his thoughts, it seemed. The reality they faced was so horribly immense it would take time to properly unfold. This island was no longer a holding area. It was their life. One by one, the implications of this would dawn on them, and, one by one, the enormity of the problem would overwhelm them.

Walking up the sloping beach, Hugo said, "I know this man. His name is Blanc."

"And this one?" Clarion asked. He made a genuine effort to hide his despair. *How can God be so cruel to Christian men?* It was not right of God to do this to them. The ship had to have gone down close to the island. How close had it occurred? And how?

Hugo shook his head. "Another cabin boy, like Blanc," he said. "I never associated with him."

The Galion de Guise *went into the sea*, Clarion thought. *It's rotting on the ocean floor.* There was almost humor in it being so close, but to laugh at such a thing would be to lose one's mind. He knew that. He'd seen it. He made the decision to remain centered, to draw inward and not give in to such desires.

"We've been waiting for a lost ship," he muttered, struggling to keep his balance in the sliding sand. The boy, though light, tested the muscles of his back.

When the Carib crawled in from the sea, only his shape remained. In the depths, down where sunlight never reached, Lonu had fashioned a careful imitation. He'd even mimicked the weight of the bones.

The ghost men hauled crates and barrels to the shoreline, sending out small boats from the great ship. With disregard, men trampled on sacred sand. They shouted into the temple of the jungle. Their swords glinted in the sun. One man climbed, disfiguring palms, collecting leaves. Others stood talking in a strange, garbled mess of a language, the racket of birds.

The man who spotted the Carib first was elderly, with a long white beard and an absurd war helmet on his head. The old man straightened in fear, and then he shouted for others. Soon the strange ghost men encircled the Carib. They prodded him with blades, shouting more, growing angry that he didn't understand.

With a heavy boot, one of the men kicked the Carib in the back of the knee, forcing him to the sand. With a sheathed hand, the man grabbed the Carib's wet hair, exposing the pulse at his neck. The old man, with a blade in one hand and a cross in the other, approached. He pointed out to the sea, presumably at other, less sacred, islands.

The Carib imitation endured the abuse, as it had been instructed to do. It felt no pain.

"*Corpus Christi,*" Denys said, offering two pieces of sugar apple, fragrant and thin as wafers. He'd cut the fruit with his heirloom dagger, one he'd brought on the voyage for comfort and memories. Hugo held an iron cross over the old man's shoulder, a gift from Captain la Reynie (a man presumably either dead or adrift) upon departure from the island. This was a pageant the two men enacted daily, one which they now performed for the survivors. With Denys' beard and frantic tension in his features, he probably looked like God to the cabin boys.

Blanc and his companion, a boy whom Perrault identified as Gabriel Monlaur, had slept through the day. After having fresh water poured down their throats, and having vomited up the same, exhaustion claimed them. They'd slept in a death state, two husks, until awakened ten hours later. Without water, Clarion knew, the boys would die. In a hut built by the crew of the *Galion de Guise* before departure, a thin structure with palm leaves for a roof, Clarion stood with a tin cup in his hand.

Outside, the sun lowered into the sea like melted copper. The worst heat of the day was gone. The jungle was already dark, garish in its nightly racket. Perrault was building a fire to chase away bloodsucking mosquitos.

Blanc took both wafers, while Monlaur, as was his habit, looked on. The cabin boy (he could've been no older than sixteen) looked at the slivers in his hand, holding them as if weighing them, and looked up at Denys, confused. His eyes were dry, matte as old leather, and sunken into his skull like withered fruit. Patches of hair were missing from his head, and his skin was red and blistered, peeling in distressingly thick layers. The new skin below was glossy, the texture of scars. He looked like he'd passed through a fire. Monlaur looked no better, another exhumed corpse.

"Partake," Denys instructed. He made the motion of eating. "It's good for your soul." He pointed up through the ceiling at God. "Don't you remember?"

"Even natives aren't confused by that," Hugo said. Disgusted, he lowered his cross and placed it atop a sea chest.

"Their brains are cooked," Clarion said, although he shared Hugo's distaste. "How they're alive, I don't know."

Denys took Blanc's hand and guided it towards the boy's parched mouth. "Open up," he said. "Open your mouth."

Blanc pursed his crumbling lips.

"What about wine?" Denys asked. "Do you remember?"

"He doesn't need wine," Clarion said. He moved Denys out of the way and offered the cup of water. Blanc declined, shaking his head, and Monlaur stared. "I'm sitting this here. There's a barrel of water in the corner. It's safe to drink. Do you understand?"

Nothing.

My sympathy only goes so far, Clarion thought. *You should be dead anyway.* "Come outside," he told Denys and Hugo. "I want to talk to you."

The three men left the cabin boys behind in the hut, pushing through the rickety gate that served as an entrance to the structure. The ocean breeze cooled their faces. The sun dipped fast here, with little twilight. As if performed with a shutter, day became night. Stars emerged above. The face of a gibbous moon shone on the water. Perrault's fire had blossomed, and he was feeding it with fuel from the tree line as the three men approached.

"How goes it?" Perrault asked. He had been sobbing. His face was swollen. Everyone knew the feeling—each had taken his turn at breaking down today.

"They're ghosts," Denys said. "Heathen ghosts at that. Neither would take communion."

Hugo, who had walked out to the beach and then returned, said, "I wonder what the Carib thinks about all this?"

The fire surged and grew tall. Perrault kept feeding it dry leaves and bark, meticulously adding slivers. He looked like he was ready to burst into tears again.

Clarion, the flames reflecting in his eyes, said, "They won't drink water. They must be dying."

"Have they spoken?" Perrault asked.

"Not a word," Clarion said. "Blanc nods every now and then."

Denys said, "They look dead already. To Hell with them. It just means one thing for us. The ship went down. The crew is gone. I presume no one knows we're here. We're in no better shape than they."

"For the time being," Clarion said, emptily. *This island may be bustling with activity in five years*, he thought. *We could be standing in a royal port.* The idea of five years almost buckled his knees. It took fortitude to face such a thought. "I need to take a walk," he said. "Either they drink or they don't. They're not infants." *Their lives are a burden to us anyway.*

The men nodded in agreement. Denys was the first to take his usual seat by the fire. He looked hard into the blaze and was alone then, too. He made no effort to read his book of psalms that night.

Clarion walked to the hut and checked inside. Blanc and Monlaur were on a bed of burlap sacks, and they appeared to be sleeping. Their breathing was noiseless. Quietly, he lifted a sword from the corner by the door, and then he was out again, walking away from the fire towards the quagmire at the jungle's edge.

He considered burying his head in the wet sand.

On another shore, distant beyond the eyes of the Frenchmen, the Caribs gathered. Canoes went into the water, filling the bay. Boys mingled among the warriors. The force was the largest the islanders could muster. All that remained now was a sign.

Beyond the canoes, another lost soul with a rope around his leg waited on a raft. The second sacrifice. When the boy went below, it would be time to proceed. Few spoke. All watched, deeply grateful for the intervention and aid of Lonu. The is-

land was his, after all. The Caribs only sought to be fine stewards.

With his back on the warm stone, the sword across his chest, his feet dangling at the edge of the cliff, and the Carib watching the sea at his side, Clarion looked at the sky, tracing shapes. He was drifting in and out of sleep, turning uncomfortably at intervals. An old memory of his wife, the look on her face when she received a birthday gift, had come to him, and he'd yet to recover. Smoke from Perrault's fire below teased his nostrils but had lessened with the passing hours. The moon had passed its midnight position. Insects, untroubled by a smoke thin as gauze, probed his neck and hands, darting and pricking.

The rhythmic tide lulled him, reminding him of nights aboard ship when the barracks had been too hot, when he'd slept on the open deck. *All those men,* he thought, *lost.* He ran through a litany of faces, a knot growing in his throat. Ninety or more men. He wondered if others, like Blanc and Monlaur, managed to secure a vessel. He'd heard stories of men in rafts, though. With no bow or stern, there was no bearing, so the ocean looked the same in every direction—sometimes the raft moved sideways, sometimes forward. It would be a slow and agonizing hell. Then dead-eyed sharks would zero in, circling. How cooked would one's brain have to be to not feel elation at hitting land after such a trial? There had been no joy in the eyes of Blanc and Monlaur.

His own feelings elbowed away the grief he felt for the others. He couldn't maintain sympathy. He'd give anything for a ship now—to be on the Atlantic, heading home. He wondered how long it would be before his sisters would make his grave in the family mausoleum. His name would be etched below his parents', beside that of his wife and above the nameless infant who had preceded him. *If I ever return, I'd enter a world where I was already dead, already mourned, my property divided and consumed.* The world could heal around one's absence like a scar. It was impossible to recover from such a realization.

Clarion sat up and scooted closer to the edge of the cliff. He placed the sword on the rocks. With the Carib, he looked out. *I'm not soulless like you,* he thought, lifting the skull. *Your kind has it easier than we do. You're like dogs. You forget your losses. God wouldn't give paradise to something more intelligent than pigs.* Before he could devolve into Hugo and have a conversation with the thing, movement at the edge of the beach caught his eye.

You're lapsing, watchman, he thought.

He was quiet as he placed the skull on the rock again, as if the sound would carry so far. He even stilled his breath. Wind and salt from the sea passed through him.

Blanc and Monlaur walked the beach, their only noise the shuffle of feet in sand. They waded into the dark water. When their hips were submerged, they stopped. Cupping their hands, the boys drank from the ocean, swallowing mouthfuls of brine. Insatiably, they drank. They swallowed enough seawater to poison a man, and they drank that way for several minutes.

Clarion pulled back from the edge of the cliff. He lay prostrate upon his stomach to hide himself, and he looked out. It occurred to him that he wanted to see Blanc and Monlaur commit suicide in the water. Delirium made the idea just.

Movement disturbed the water around them. Clarion strained to see, but the moon was faint, and the men were forty yards distant. The water rippled around their hands, as if a fish fed at their fingertips below the surface. Blanc and Monlaur went to their knees, then dipped their heads. They remained under for minutes. The ridge of a spine, sharp as a fin, emerged, breaking the surface between them. A third figure had entered in the water. Oily scales covered the spine. When Blanc and Monlaur raised their heads, water streaming around their patchy skulls, another face lifted.

Clarion's blood cooled.

The face was not human, but there was something emotive about it. Two small eyes, glazed and clouded black, set at outward angles at the edges of the face. The skull was long and thin. The creature had an impossibly large mouth, which hinged at the base of the head and filled with water as it gulped. The mouth was large enough to fit over a man's ribcage. Long gills at the side of the neck excreted dark water, flowing with the consistency of blood. A snakelike tail whipped, powerfully, and the creature submerged again. Clarion was not able to determine whether the thing had legs or fins beneath its bulk. He saw no more. The creature was gone, leaving Blanc and Monlaur alone.

Clarion's first inclination was that of a brute animal: if the boys were near he'd hack them with his sword. Such emotion was a counterpoint to terror, friction in the face of paralysis. He realized this. He tried to be calm, to find his center. The abomination was deeper, though, disturbing at the level of the soul.

Blanc and Monlaur, after stealing a few more drinks, trudged from the brine. They moved like mechanical things, unaware of anything outside their skulls. They did not look around for fear of being seen. They did not speak to one another, save for one word that drifted through darkness.

Lonu, Blanc said.

He said the word once and only once, as though it were necessary. Something had changed in their gait: there was strength where pallor and death had been before. Blanc and Monlaur were coming to life.

Clarion moved farther from the edge and stood. He lifted his sword from the rock. Although he tried to smother the creature's image in his thoughts, it was foremost. He soon had difficulty separating imagination from what he had truly seen. Did the creature have haunches below its tail? Did it plant feet in the sand or did it float? He walked to the trail that led to the beach below. Heavy with dread, his knuckles were white above the pommel of his rapier.

The trail opened into darkness, like an extended jaw. His presence brought unnatural silence to the jungle, and when he moved on the din replaced him. He passed through as quickly as he could manage, his bare feet skirting wriggling life at the edge of the quagmire. He held his sword at the ready. The dying flames of Perrault's fire guided him. When he reached the sand, he saw Blanc and Monlaur on the ground beside the fire. Denys, Hugo, and Perrault were nowhere in sight. Perhaps they had gone to sleep in the hut. He approached, sword in his grip. Blanc and Monlaur were asleep or pretending to sleep. They looked peaceful. Clarion considered running his sword through each, but he hesitated. He doubted.

He trudged through sand to the water line. The tide came in peacefully. Nothing unnatural or foreign occupied the dark water. He slashed at the brine, and the effect produced nothing. He wiped the blade on the baggy, ripped cloth of his breeches. He waited, torn. He questioned his sight, his mind, but he knew he was not losing his grasp like Denys. He had seen what he had seen.

What brought the two of you out here? he thought. *Why are you not sleeping in the hut?* Then more sinister questions occurred to him. He looked back at Blanc and Monlaur. Again he considered running them through.

What are you? What brought you here?

Denys, as he chose to do sometimes, sported his war helmet in the morning. His voice woke Clarion. The old man was singing a children's song, something he'd picked up from the streets of Paris in the old days. On he went with something about a blonde. Then, collecting a sword from the corner of the hut, said he, "Today is the day you remember." He opened the door and went out. His helmet glistened in the morning sunlight. "Up, up, heathens," he shouted. His voice grew distant, but he started on the melody again.

Clarion pressed the sleep from his eyes and stretched. The night had been long and his sleep short. He'd awakened repeatedly. His back was sore from lying upon rock. Quietly, he rose from the mat and stood. He left Hugo and Perrault. Images from the night were in his mind like knots. He still felt the tension of it all.

Clarion found Denys by the ashes, prodding at Blanc and Monlaur with his sword. *He notices nothing odd about them*, Clarion thought. The image of the thing in the water, the tail, the jaw, came to him again. It would require sorcery and glamour to imagine something so vivid, he reasoned. *Or madness*. He fought away the doubt. He had seen what he had seen. *Then*, he had to ask, *why did you not run them through?* With distrust, he approached.

"Today you remember," Denys ordered.

Blanc and Monlaur opened their eyes, wet as pools now. Much of their sun-destroyed skin had fused without scars. They were no longer the scabrous, marooned shapes that floated in from the sea only a day prior. They were, indeed, growing stronger, as Clarion had suspected. Such healing was unnatural. It was the province of miracles.

"I need to speak with you, Denys," Clarion said.

The old man turned. The single plume of egret remaining in his helmet wobbled in the breeze. Clarion had, more than once, been tempted to throw the helmet into the sea. "Where were you last night?" Denys asked.

With the old man distracted, Blanc and Monlaur inched away from the dangling blade. Clarion watched them like a warden with prisoners. He wanted to tell them how close he had been to killing them. "On the ledge with the Carib," he said. "I was a little bothered."

"Let us take communion with these heathens, and ask God to send a vessel," Denys said.

Clarion took Denys by the arm and pulled him towards the waterline. Reluctantly, Denys stepped away from his spiritual charges. The ocean moved serenely in the morning. Frigatebirds lined the shoals of the bay, long lines of black shroud. The salted breeze came in from the water. Clarion felt nothing except the turmoil of his thoughts. In blunt language, he told Denys what he had seen. He did not worry if imagination bled into reality. He told it all as he remembered it. He revealed his suspicion of Blanc and Monlaur. He left out only his hesitation in killing them. He portrayed the act as one of mercy rather than weakness.

When Clarion finished, Denys said, "Poor man, look what grief has done to you."

A large wave pushed the water halfway up the beach, leaving crabs in the wake.

"I saw it," Clarion insisted.

Denys shook his head, a gesture that, in the moment, was maddeningly arrogant. "Let us take communion, and ask God for a vessel," he repeated.

Clarion grabbed Denys and shook him, leaving the helmet lopsided, covering one eye. "Have you lost your mind?" he asked. "Will you not hear me? I need not remind you there are such things. Do you not remember our first island of Caribs? They worship devils in the water. Do you not remember their threats?" *Our Hell is in the earth*, he thought, *and theirs is out there in the water, living.*

Denys adjusted his helmet. Maybe he was fully gone now. There was something artificial in his face. "Find comfort in His flesh and His blood. Where is my rosary, Clarion? Did you take it?"

"Turn and look, you old fool," Clarion said. "There they go again."

Blanc and Monlaur had walked down the beach and entered the water. To Clarion's dismay, the duo only cleaned their faces. They did not partake of the brine. It was mundane.

"You see?" Denys asked. "Grief got the best of you." He chuckled. "Our sick commander."

Clarion stopped short of smacking the grin from Denys' face.

"Only God is in control now," Denys said.

"That's nothing to celebrate," Clarion said. He turned to walk away. "God should not have done this to us."

Although Monlaur was still walking comatose, Blanc began to converse. Nodding turned into monosyllables that turned into short strings of words. He spoke as one would if learning vocabulary, a parroting thing. He even took communion, but only in mimicry of Hugo. The skin on Blanc's head healed rapidly, healing even as one looked at him. Scabs went away in the course of a conversation. Hair grew at Blanc's crown where none had been before. Sitting in the cool sand in the shade of the hut, he answered questions from Hugo and Perrault, who had somehow won his trust. Monlaur looked on. A strange tale emerged.

The *Galion de Guise* encountered a strong windstorm at sea, but that was not what brought about the end of the ship, according to Blanc. He looked at Clarion when he said this. He let his gaze linger, as if he were probing, collecting. Clarion broke the connection, looking away. His skin crawled. Something ripped into the hull, Blanc said then, creatures with immense jaws from under the sea. He spoke of whip-like tails beating against the undergirding of the ship. Deep, ominous thudding. Sea monsters, then.

"What did they look like?" Perrault asked, as astonished as he should have been.

Blanc grew silent. He did not remember. He glanced once more at Clarion, something knowing in the look, something shared, then away into the jungle.

"Who else survived?" Hugo asked.

Blanc shook his head.

Clarion walked away. It was in his mind to go and re-trieve one of the muskets. As soon as he stepped into the hut, though, Hugo crowded in behind him. The two men were alone.

"I imagined you'd have more interest in all this," Hugo said. "You look at Blanc like you're repulsed by him."

"Is it so obvious?"

Hugo shrugged. Hemming, he asked, "What are you looking for? Denys' rosary?"

"A musket," Clarion said.

"For what purpose?"

Ingrate, Clarion thought. *Who are you to demand an answer from me?* "To shoot Blanc," he muttered. "I want to see how fast he'll heal."

Shaken, Hugo said, "Denys told us what you saw." A little adrenaline moved in his voice, gave it a tremor. He was too pathetic to abuse, as he always had been.

Clarion had to laugh. "The world is turned upside down," he said. "You take Denys' word over mine. His is the voice of reason." He found the war helmet among Denys' belongings. Pointing, he said, "This is whom you listen to."

"I think—"

"—What is it that you think, child? Enlighten me."

Tears wailed in Hugo's eyes. He acted as one raised by women, without a man in his life, as he always had. "I think your heart is broken," Hugo managed to say. "Like all of us. Do not turn your rage on those men. They've already suffered."

Clarion swallowed his emotion. It took great will to not give in to the grief Hugo openly displayed. "I'm going hunting then," Clarion said. "Blanc is safe from me." There was a tremble in his voice now, but he fought it. This was the second time he'd turned from killing the man.

Hugo openly wept. "We'll never see home," he said. "My—"

"—Do not trouble me with this," Clarion said. "You've made your point well enough." He found one of the muskets. He retrieved a paper cartridge, just a single ball and powder. Even a marksman would be distressed by the futility of just one, but Clarion hadn't the energy to search for more.

Hugo took a seat on the ground. He covered his face, ashamed.

Clarion stormed out, his mind a blur.

He'd been walking ceaselessly for hours, trying not to think or remember, failing at both. The sun was growing low when he saw the first of them. Clarion stopped mid-stride, cradling the musket. The sword jangled against his leg. Mosquitoes attacked. He was near a freshwater spring, a beautiful oasis, where water trickled from the edge of a cliff side. Tropical flowers, vibrant with color, erupted from the soil. Vines snaked, devouring every surface. The spring fed a small pool, a glistening hole of water that led into a cave below. Clarion saw the thing from the corner of his eye. A barbed tail slithered along the top of the water like a snake, and then it went below. He had not been imagining. The tail left behind wide ripples.

The horror of invasion came to him. Months on the island had given him a sense of ownership. Immediately, Clarion turned and started back along the trail. He was far from the beach, however. He'd positively sabotaged himself, leaving his return journey for the dark. The sun dipped, and it was night. He walked for two more hours, forgetting his exhaustion, his deep hunger, thinking only of his anger and horror. It was when he approached the quagmire, so close now, that he saw the second of them. The edge of a jaw ruptured the wet sand. Dark grit lay over the teeth.

He kept on. When he reached the white beach, he stopped cold. Blanc and Monlaur stood at the edge of firelight, shadows across their faces, staring down at the sleeping form of Hugo. Denys and Perrault, presumably, were in the hut. Hugo slept alone, for a reason only he knew, his feet towards the low fire, while Blanc and Monlaur observed him.

Blanc held the sun-bleached Carib skull.

Clarion froze, unseen in the shadow of the palms.

Writhing, coiling like a snake around a lance, a long, barbed tail moved down Monlaur's leg. The tail extended onto the ground, slowly inching, creating a ridge in the sand as it progressed. Soon the tail lay across Hugo's neck, like a wire garroting a criminal. The barb entered his flesh, burrowing. Blood moved in the rhythm of a heartbeat from the wound, spurting once around the tail, and then oozing. Hugo opened his mouth, as if to scream, but he only vomited blood. The tail went deeper, probing, eventually emerging through his mouth, like a hook snaring a fish. Monlaur turned and dragged Hugo towards the sea. He dragged the man with ease.

Blanc, with the Carib skull in his hand, followed.

Clarion shook himself from the stupor. He threw aside his musket and lifted his sword. He charged, but it was all for naught. He had not seen the thing that fully emerged, covered in sand, from the quagmire. While mesmerized, another tail had coiled around Clarion's leg. He fell hard against the ground, having the presence of mind only to release his sword in a forward motion. Blanc, Monlaur, and Hugo went into the tide. There was nothing Clarion could do. He landed on his stomach, knocking air from his body. He gasped for breath and tried to turn. He managed only a glimpse before the world went black. It was the face he had seen in the tide, the impossible mouth, and the same he'd seen in the morass. The jaw gaped in a poor imitation of breathing. The tail uncoiled from his leg and darted upward, piercing the side of his face. The barb entered like a blade.

Clarion awoke on the beach, the sun white in his eyes, sweat mingling with sand in his beard. The muscles in his neck and shoulders felt as though they had ossified. For a moment, the slightest uncanny second, he believed he looked into the face of God, but it was only Denys. The old man was on his knees in the sand, shaking Clarion, saying something frantic. He held the rosary now. It was just a blur of noise for Clarion. He managed to sit up, and his head throbbed like he'd been drinking all night. His sword lay in the sand, not far from the ashes of the fire.

"Gone," Denys was saying, his voice a refrain.

Memories of the night came in a rush. Clarion recoiled. "Who is gone?" he asked. His voice was dry like scraping gravel.

"The heathens," he said. "And Hugo."

"What about Perrault?"

"He's looking for Hugo. He went into the jungle."

Clarion cupped his head, fighting the pain.

"I couldn't stop him. He insisted. They were children together."

Clarion drew a trilling breath. "Hugo's not in the jungle," he said. "I saw. Monlaur killed him."

"Then they're still here. There's nowhere to go other than inland."

Clarion looked over his shoulder at the sea. "Out there," he said.

A shout from Perrault halted them. He was on the rock outcropping, a swirl of fog from the jungle at his back. "More rafts," he shouted.

Clarion got to his feet. His legs were like rubber, but with the aid of Denys he moved towards the water. There was tremendous swelling at the edge of his mouth and along his jawline. His face was numb, the vision in his left eye blurred, as if something had stung him. He recalled the barbed tail then.

In the distance, dark shapes covered the sea. Perrault was a fool. The shapes did not move like rafts, and they did not move like boats from a ship. The shapes moved like canoes. Hundreds and hundreds of canoes.

"Caribs," Denys said. Stoically, he adjusted his helmet. "I'll fetch the arms."

"They have the skull, your watchman," Clarion remarked.

Indeed, on the end of a pike, a native held the blank skull aloft. Near to this, a shredded body, just a trunk without legs or arms or head, bridged another set of pikes: the uneaten remains, Clarion fathomed, of poor Hugo. Meat hung like petals from the cage of bones. Clarion steeled himself.

"At least we found the rosary," Denys said. "That is a sign. God will deliver us."

Clarion shut his eyes. He didn't speak for fear of damning himself.

A chant, a refrain, rose from the Caribs. Clarion recognized a single word: *Lonu.*

The wave of invasion had finally come.

"Canoes," Perrault was screaming now. "Canoes!"

THE FOURTH IMPOSTOR:

SIRE
of the
HATCHET

It looked more like a child.

The mound drew him. Hutter stopped in the road so suddenly that his companion walked ten paces before noticing. The companion, too, then stopped and turned, but his eyes were glazed and tired rather than curious. He reminded Hutter of the lateness of the hour, of their destination. His face was drawn and pinched, vitriolic.

"Something crawled from the hillock," Hutter whispered, cautious of his voice in the surrounding forest. It dawned on him that neither he nor his assistant had spoken in several hours. The road seemed nothing more than a vein in a vast body here, hidden once, but now teased to the fore and blue. Was it days of travel that infected him? *You're seeing things,* he thought.

"Codswallop," the companion, a rogue named Wolfric, said.

Hutter placed his satchel on the dirt. He drew the hatchet from the twine at his waist and gripped a handle laced with carvings. He moved into the shadow of the overhanging trees. It was summer, and the canopy was thick. The cool wind from the tree line felt anything but pleasant, however. The forest was alive with the chatter of insects and the stench of rotten vegetation.

Wolfric, a nervous man without provocation, was at his side now, a dagger longer than his hand in his grip. "A highwayman?" he asked. God knows he'd feared such a happening for the entirety of the journey. As the companion of an executioner, Wolfric had a head full of stories. If there were a time when he believed all men were human, it had been before he made the acquaintance of Hutter. And with executioners, there was always the specter of revenge.

"It looked more like a child," Hutter said.

"You need an axe for a child?" Wolfric, mercurial, now laughed.

"It *looked* like a child."

"Why don't we get on, then?"

Hutter found himself being honest. "I don't know," he admitted. After all, the mound drew him. There was something magnetic in its pulse. With that, he stepped through a ditch and moved towards the mound, while Wolfric remained on the road. Hutter mashed dead leaves, causing a racket. He stood out, a lumbering oaf with a blade, but he couldn't help himself. The mound looked too small, too well-shaped, to be natural. It stood only ten feet from the floor of the forest. If man-made, he surmised, thinking of his home in Saxony where there were similar mounds, then this was what his father called one of the old fairy doors. The ancestors of man, heathens of filth, erected similar mounds to worship devils. His father, a member of the Pietist sect of the Lutheran faith, was colorful in his hatred for pagans. *Ours is a curious heritage,* Hutter thought, stepping still closer. *We reject it and admire it.* From what he had heard on the coast, Indians across the sea built mounds, too. *Cathedrals of filth,* he thought, *but everyone is drawn to them.*

What had he seen crawl from the knoll? Was it more than a shadow show? A feeling with depth, akin to dread, spread inside. Now so close to the mound, he faced the real question. Could a tangle of roots scuttle forth like an infant?

Hutter circled the mound, hatchet at the ready, but found nothing except leaves and lances of sunlight.

Gnats swarmed his head every moment he stopped. He circled twice, but he was cautious not to touch, let alone climb, the mound. The only smell was that of raw earth, pleasing rather than threatening.

Wolfric stood on the road in sunlight, cupping his hand against his mouth, shouting things about the hour.

A fetus of roots, Hutter thought. *An abomination.* God, how it appeared so clearly in his mind. "It's nothing," he called out. "Branches," he said. "Shadows." The words stuck in his throat.

Hutter made his way again, still gripping the hatchet, toward the road, the only thoroughfare to the village of his calling. His destination was a hamlet of the English called Strattonwick. His duty was that of an executioner.

Suffering is holy.

Strattonwick hung like a broken jaw above the generous floodplain, disjointed and cockeyed, strewn across two hillsides. The village possessed the symmetry of an unexpected heave, of something disgorged. This was one of the old communal villages, a relic of serfdom with everything shared by the inhabitants and everything owned by the local Earl. The people lived more like employees than inhabitants of the estate. The plain abutted the branch of a dark river, and vegetables grew plentiful in the field's rich soil. Men with beaten utensils moved between the rows, swatting insects that delighted in their sweat. A single road skirted the gardens, winding up the hillside on one end and disappearing into a forest on the other. The road was empty of traffic save for two bedraggled strangers on foot. The sun was nearly down, so shadows moved in the branches, deepening the gloom. The moon was faintly visible in the sky. Mosquitoes and bats swarmed the slow-moving river.

It was rumored in Strattonwick that a single wolf had somehow found its way into the forest again. This made the men of the village alert. Sometimes men stayed up nights and listened for the predator, but it was never seen. The men in the gardens did see the travelers, however, and they stopped their work, standing erect and staring at the intrusion of strangers.

Wolfric sneered at Hutter. How he hated his fellow man. Hutter adjusted his satchel and kept his pace. Instinctively, he touched the hatchet at his waist. He understood men like these villagers, petty and defensive folk who talked honor and dishonor while grubbing in the earth, and who watched all strangers like they were wolves in a nursery. "Chin up," he told Wolfric. "We'll be leaving the richer."

"I'd like to smash them all with the back end of an axe." His face went red as blood, and the veins of hard drinking emerged along his nose.

Hutter shook his head. Unlike Wolfric, he accepted his place in the world. Maybe it was because his father, too, had been an executioner. As a boy, he'd learned how men treated those in the dishonorable trades. His own sons would face the same looks and derision one day. Wolfric claimed a higher descent than Hutter, although this was dubious. His family, too, was scum, his father a mercenary.

Three men emerged from the gardens and walked to the road. Each of the men held a hoe as if it were a cudgel, and each tried to ignore the insects at their shoulders and necks. Occasionally, a hand went up in defense, but it was an act begrudged. Hutter stopped Wolfric, observing a custom he'd learned while still a journeyman. From his satchel, he retrieved the papers that identified him as a master in the trade. The men, though they certainly could not read, would demand to see papers. Then they would make a show of letting their eyes linger, full of consternation, on what appeared to be meaningless curls and tangles. Custom transcended education. Theirs was not an exercise in scrutiny, but a bluffing game of cat and mouse.

When the two groups met at the base of an incline, all was silent save for the chorus of frogs on the shore and the drone of insects in the woods. The men smelled of oxen feces, which was more or less the clay of their art. "We're here for the girl," Hutter said. He offered the papers, pressed with the signature of his father, the man to whom, so many years ago, he'd apprenticed.

There was not an elder among the villagers. All three of the men were youthful, the age of new fathers. The man who'd accepted the papers stepped closer, separating himself. He had a dirt-scarred face and a bulbous nose. He was balding, save for a shock of blond hair at the crown of his head. He spoke with the gait of an imbecile. He was not one to be mocked, though. He was thick in the shoulders and possessed hands like granite. He looked like he could tear a man's arm out by the roots, and had.

"They're waiting," he said. "You go ask for Master Croft. You show him this."

Hutter took back the papers and nodded. The men turned towards the field, and they whispered to one another. *Sentinels*, he thought.

"And he was the best of them," Wolfric said. "The spokesman."

"I notice you waited 'til he was gone to say that."

"I'm only a fool when I drink," he said.

Hutter and Wolfric walked up the hillside. This branch of the forest road ended with a smattering of thatched-roof hovels and stone chimneys. Women, children, and old men moved about the structures, navigating a series of roiling cauldrons. Oxen moved about with relative freedom, like pet dogs. A fenced sty kept pigs at bay. The only building with any multi-generational permanence was the Strattonwick church house, built with cut planks and fortified with river stones. Still, even this structure was barren, lacking ornamentation. The church was squat and gray and sturdy, and it stood beside a stall of milking cows.

An elder waited at the door of the church, looking pensive. Despite the evening heat, he wore the heavy brown coat of a Puritan. Beneath his hat, his gray hair was cut like a bowl, another mark of his inclination. He was an austere man, judging by the look on his face. He glanced up, revealing a grizzled visage, scarred by a sword thrust at his cheek. One of his hands was missing, and the skin at his wrist was slick and shining. He was once a soldier, Hutter surmised.

"We're looking for Master Croft," Hutter said. Wolfric, tense, stood silently at his side.

"I'm Croft," the old man said. He reached out and accepted the papers offered. With a succinct, educated manner, he scanned the document. He covered Hutter and Wolfric with a quick look, too, stopping a moment on the exposed hatchet at Hutter's waist and the dagger at Wolfric's. "Very well," he said. "Master Hutter, welcome. And your companion?"

"Wolfric Blum, my assistant."

"Master Blum," Croft said. "I'm Israel Croft, the pastor here in Strattonwick. The schoolteacher and magistrate for Lord Allingham, likewise. This is my mission," he said, almost defensively. Then he drank in the smoky, putrid air of the village. Godly intentions, he seemed to say, were nothing about which one should be embarrassed.

"Suffering is holy," Wolfric observed wryly.

Israel Croft could send a man to Hell with his glance, and he let it linger on Wolfric.

Jesus, Hutter thought. Croft, a man of fire and brimstone, possessed no humor.

"Come into the church," Croft said finally. "You can sleep here, but nowhere else. I cannot invite you to my home, you understand. It would be dishonorable. It wouldn't be proper. And there's no inn."

"Indeed, it wouldn't," Hutter said. He did his best to pretend the rebuke had no impact.

The three men walked into the church. It was musty and hot, dark from a lack of windows.

"I'll introduce you to the quarry in the morning," Croft said. "We'll pay you to interrogate her. Then, of course, we'll pay for what follows."

"That's understood," Hutter said.

With that, Croft began showing the executioners around his meager church. When it was too dark to see, he lit a precious candle stub and extended the flame with his quivering hand. He promised to pray for their souls. That, too, would be part of their pay. He offered the men the "Harlot Pews" at the back of the church for sleeping.

When the night was full, he personally brought the executioners two bowls of gruel (one at a time, of course, considering the limitations of his hand).

"I could never understand Puritans," Wolfric said. He sat alone in the front pew rather than the back, his muddy boots resting on the wood.

Hutter, bothered, paced the main aisle. The planks were loose and noisy. "You're not arrogant enough to understand Puritans," he said. "You have to be sure you're going to Heaven and everyone else is going to Hell to understand them."

"Is that all?"

"About all. You also have to have the right name."

Wolfric laughed. "Chosen at birth then. You think his name is really Israel?"

"I once knew a Puritan who named his children Fear-Sin, Praise-God, and Wrestling-Evil. Poor chaps."

"Damn cult is what they are."

Hutter couldn't disagree.

I saw it, too.

In the complete darkness of the church, stretched on the hard pews, Hutter tried to sleep, but his mind kept wandering to the mound he'd spied earlier in the day. He turned from shoulder to shoulder, rustling the blanket draped across his legs. Fear, of which he was not proud, grew in his heart. He thought of his own sons, boys who complained of things in the dark. *Shameful,* he thought, *for a man to feel this way.*

Wolfric, in the pew directly ahead, stirred, as well. His voice, when it came out of the darkness, was not unwelcome. From what he asked, it was clear he, too, was thinking of the mound.

"What'd you see today?" Wolfric asked. The two men had not spoken for hours, and now this.

Hutter turned the question over in his mind. "You're wanting honesty."

"I am." Wolfric had to be deep in thought to be so solemn. Something ate at him.

The image had not left Hutter's mind. He knew it well. "Tree roots shaped like an infant, like bones arranged in a skeleton. It moved from the mound."

"It crawled, didn't it?" Wolfric asked.

"It crawled out of the mound. I saw it no more, though."

Wolfric breathed deeply. For several minutes, he said nothing. Wind, the front of a budding thunderstorm, moved through the plank walls, trembling the wood and whistling through stone. The change of air made the cows outside the wall stir and complain. Hutter was prepared to let the matter drop and try for sleep again.

"I saw it, too," Wolfric said.

This was not the stability Hutter had sought when answering the question. He wanted to be rebuked for his childishness. He had no desire for affirmation. "On the mound?" The wind became something physical in his mind then, and he started with every sigh the storm caused in the darkness.

"After. It was following us along the road, crawling in the trees."

"Following us? Why?" Hutter had been careful not to touch the mound, and he said as much.

Wolfric did not offer an answer. Neither he nor Hutter dared say what was on their mind. The matter went below, yet it remained a barrier to their sleep.

She drowned the child in earth.

"Witchcraft," Israel Croft said. "Witches are the Devil's soldiers, and this girl is no less." The Puritan led the executioners through Strattonwick. He was no stranger to having a captive audience, and he treated Hutter and Wolfric as such. He couldn't help but to preach, even in response to simple questions. He prattled on about witches and Satan.

The villagers were up with the morning sun, surveying the damage of a quick thunderstorm that had rushed through prior to dawn. The sky was clear now, and the air was humid, thick. Birds made a racket as they flew down to the river. When the executioners passed, the villagers looked away, lest they be tainted. It was a ritual these people had learned from their parents. The gesture, in their minds at least, somehow inoculated them against dishonor. Not even poor folk, not even the rogues who hauled human shit to the gardens or carried squawking chickens by their feet to the slaughter, felt akin to Hutter and Wolfric. The strangers were as good as outlaws. No one bothered to greet the men who had arrived with the sole intention of doing Strattonwick's dirty work. To even look at them was anathema.

Croft went on. "I've no doubt Rosamond dabbled in such things. She was no woman of the church. No one ever called her goodwife by mistake." At this, he chuckled. It was a dry, ugly laugh. "She was a heathen of the forest."

"I hate Puritans," Wolfric muttered. It was no empty remark. He'd had other run-ins with their kind in Saxony.

Croft rubbed his face with the nub of his left wrist, a motion that probably appeared as unnatural and frightening as a scarecrow to children. He was such a thin wraith of a man.

"Witchcraft is not the reason you're here, as you know." The comment had the ring of disappointment. "Rosamond murdered her child when it was but a newborn." He stopped and turned. "That much you know. There's more to it. She drowned the child in earth," he said. The minister paused, allowing the gravity of this to sink in.

Hutter found the idea repulsive. It was, in his mind, the worst of the crimes he encountered. The perpetrator was worthy of a hard death. He thought of his sons and wife. He couldn't fathom the depth of such an act. He grimaced.

"She stuffed dirt in the boy's mouth until he choked. She clamped his mouth with the palm of her hand. Drowned in his own body." Croft's eyes widened. "Then she buried him in the woods. Thank God one of the local girls saw her. No one ever even knew Rosamond was pregnant. She showed no signs. Satan can manipulate what we see, though. Then again, she came and went. I believe the heathen begged on the forest road. Probably sold her flesh."

Rattled, Hutter asked, "She hasn't confessed?"

"The threat of Hell didn't sway her," Croft admitted. "We're hoping your tools will. Of course, with a witness, a confession isn't fully necessary. The drowning will go on tomorrow, regardless. Yet a confession would make things cleaner for the Earl, Lord Allingham. What with a young girl being the witness. Women lie, as you're no doubt aware. Products of the weak Eve. I'd like you to work her over today, see what you can extract."

"We'd like to see her," Hutter said.

"We'll start now," Wolfric added.

Croft nodded.

A rudely constructed shed, built from scrap, roofed with insect-ridden thatch, housed Rosamond. At the rear of the village, on an incline where the hill started upward again, the shed was largely removed from the daily bustle. The forest loomed over the structure, casting shadows. Thick dew covered the surrounding weeds. Normally, the shed housed garden tools, but now it was a jail. A young man with a cudgel stood guard at the entrance. The boy stepped aside as Croft approached. He looked away when Hutter greeted him.

"It stinks of her," Croft said. "Gird yourself." He removed a cross bar and pulled open the door. The shed was dark on the inside, save for a few lances of sunlight that pierced gaps in the walls. The interior stank of earth, sweat, and urine. When Croft called to the girl, his voice deepened with authority. Hutter wondered if the Puritan had commanded when he was a soldier. He had the natural air. "Rosamond Wise," he said. "Stand, girl."

Hutter moved closer for a better look.

Rosamond was a pitiful sight. She stood from the dirt on wobbly, malnourished legs. She was thin as ropes and just as unsteady. She looked like a starved dog. Life had left her eyes, leaving an abyss in her clouded gaze. She wore a burlap sack for a dress and nothing more. Her feet were bare and blackened. Her hair, dark as ink, hung in knotted clumps, and dry mud braided the locks. Her mouth was a thin line, betraying no feeling. Her nose was wide and swollen and discolored where she'd been struck with a fist. The bruises spread into her eyes.

"Looks like you already worked her over," Wolfric said.

She isn't strong enough to torture, Hutter thought. Then he forced himself to remember her crime. Again, he pictured his children. If dispassionate, he could never do his job well. Anger was a must. He won Croft's respect by taunting the girl.

"Shall we have a talk?" he asked.

Rosamond, as if her eyes were painted stones, looked ahead without seeing, emotionless. Though she was a young woman, her hands trembled like those of the elderly. She was ready to die.

"It can't be done in there," Wolfric told Croft. "We need space."

"Of course," Croft said, a little offended by the assumption. "We've prepared a spot for you in the woods." Cruelly, he looked at Rosamond. "I'd hate for her screams to disturb the womenfolk."

"Doesn't look like she speaks or screams," Wolfric said.

"She screams," Croft remarked.

Hatchet the roots, wither the tree.

Where Strattonwick met the forest, a thin trail began its labyrinthine route. The trail was wide enough for a single horse and rider, no more. *Walk the trail far enough and you'll end up at the stables of Lord Allingham,* Croft had said, noticeably proud of his lord. The Puritan, bedecked in coat and wide-brimmed hat, led Hutter and Wolfric to a clearing a few hundred yards from the village. There was a scummy pond here, crowned with the refuse of frogs, and there was a pad of trimmed grass surrounded by primeval oak trees. *Our little oasis*, Croft had said. *Idyllic.* Then, as if a busy man, he left the executioners with Rosamond. The Puritan whistled as he went away on the trail, a tuneless hymn, but soon the cavernous forest ate up his melody. It was as if he were making a point.

Rosamond, wrists and ankles bound with hemp, backed awkwardly against one of the oaks and slid to the ground. She had yet to make a noise.

"What do you make of Croft?" Hutter asked.

Wolfric shook his head. "One of the truer bastards I've met. Too bad war didn't take more than his hand."

Hutter chuckled. "He'd say God spared him."

"Of course he would. What would the world do without Israel Croft? How would this pile of shit function without his one steady hand and guidance? Reminds me of my time in the lowlands. Did I ever tell you—"

"—He's no soldier." The voice was so alien and unexpected that both Hutter and Wolfric turned, startled.

Rosamond stared forward, still and emotionless, and said no more. It came to Hutter then that the woman never blinked. An odd detail, yet there it was.

"I'll be damned," Wolfric said. "I'll get a fire ready."

Hutter walked to the woman's side and knelt. He had the sick feeling that this woman was capable of lurching and biting him. There was something of the wild animal in her. Still, he remained at her side.

"What do you know of Master Croft?" he asked. "What do you make of him? Could it be he chopped off his hand to see what was inside?" This was, he would admit, a highly unusual approach to a quarry one was prepared to put through the pain of torture, but the entire journey had been odd. Strattonwick was odd.

Rosamond did not answer. Being so close to her was like being at the wake of a corpse. Vegetable life was the only life in this woman. *No spirit,* he thought.

Hutter, out of an unwieldy fear more than wisdom, let his next question die without expression. It was irrational, and he chastised himself for the thought. He wanted to ask the woman about the mound he'd seen on the forest road, of the sticks moving in the shape of an infant. Why that had come to him, he could not say, but Rosamond inspired the same feelings the mound inspired. She drew him now. The gravity of Rosamond's presence could wither a man's bravado.

Wolfric, eager, had already gone to work building a small fire. Diligently, he raked flint. Soon, smoke curled around his shoulders. When the fire could sustain itself, he retrieved the iron pincers from his satchel. While smiling at Rosamond, he placed the tongs in the flame, letting the utensil roast and turn orange.

"That will happen only if you don't speak," Hutter said, in a tone he generally used on children. In a lower register, he went on. "Ol' Wolf will raise your arms up and pin them. Then he'll take the tongs and put it to your armpit. First the left. When it's hot like that, skin comes off with the slightest pinch. The right arm is next. Is that worth your silence, girl? He'll take a chunk of skin the size of a coin."

Rosamond, despite her effort, breathed heavily. The thin line at her mouth trembled. Tears rimmed her eyes. Still, she did not close them. She did not blink.

Wolfric made a show of monitoring the pincers. He gripped the tool and held it aloft, as if testing its readiness. He seemed more ogre than human, and it was an act he enjoyed. Wolfric was capable of great cruelty with his inhibitions lowered.

Rosamond's next words were almost a chant, spoken like a lyric. "You have the hatchet. Are you its sire?" Rosamond asked. She pointed to the woodsman's tool at Hutter's waist.

"What does that mean?"

"Sire of the Hatchet," Rosamond said, her voice sing-song.

"You're speaking nonsense."

Wolfric stood with the glowing pincers.

"Wait," Hutter said. Looking into Rosamond's eyes, he felt the tang of copper at the back of his throat, and an itch in his spine. The tears, when they moved over her bruises, began to change. He saw it happen. He couldn't believe it, but he saw it. The tears turned into dark fleas and leapt from her skin. Instinctively, Hutter jumped back. "What are you?" he asked.

"What's wrong?" Wolfric moved forward with the tongs. "Did she bite you? Lift her arms, damn it."

Breathing heavily, Hutter said, "Wait, I told you. Put it in the fire, Wolf."

"You've lost your mind," Wolfric said. "Or she's hexed you."

"What are you?" Hutter asked, inching forward again.

"Hatchet the roots, wither the tree. Sire of the hatchet. Cutter of the cross."

"She's playin' a witch with you," Wolfric said. When the pincers lost their glow, he placed the tool in the fire again. "You've seen her kind before. A game of the mind," he said. "No doubt that works with Master Croft, but not here, girl."

Hutter could no longer contain his question. "What of the mound?" he asked.

"Codswallop," Wolfric said.

"What of it?" he asked Rosamond.

Rosamond's blank eyes stared forward. She had not blinked, and she had not looked at Hutter. It was as if the eyes were blind imitations.

"The mother's belly," she said.

"You knew of our journey here?"

Rosamond said nothing.

"The roots?"

"The children."

"Wolf saw the roots following us."

"Indeed, he did. They're worried about me. They're with you more than you know. They were with you in the church last night."

At that, a great rustling of leaves arose from behind the oaks. The noise formed a circle around the clearing.

Wolfric dropped the pincers. "Jesus God," he said, staring into the shadows. His face went ashen.

At the brink of losing his nerve, Hutter asked, "Did you kill your child?"

"It was not my child," Rosamond said.

"Did you kill him?"

"I did not."

"Did you bury him?"

"Yes. And Croft killed him by digging him up. Croft knows," she said. "Long ago he chopped his wrist to find out. He knows."

Unabated, the forest moved around them. Hutter chanced a look behind the oaks. He saw the hard line of a root move like an arm out of sight.

"She confessed to burying it," Wolfric said. "That's enough."

Hutter agreed. He yanked the girl to a standing position. Then, without a word, he shoved her towards the trail. Unsatisfied with the pace, Wolfric lifted Rosamond and carried her back to the village.

She said nothing more. Her eyes were dry of tears.

What disturbed you, Puritan?

The site of execution was a large rock that formed a platform by the riverside. The locals, Croft said, called it the Raven Stone, naming it for the scavengers that fed on criminals here. Three sharp pikes impaled the ground beside the rock, pikes empty of heads—a reminder to those inclined towards malfeasance.

"Peasants don't come here," Croft said. "They believe it's haunted." He laughed.

"Who carved all these names?" asked Hutter. He pointed to the myriad etchings that lined the stones: names, mottos, phrases from the Bible, marks like runes.

"Brave children," Croft said. "Children dare each other to come down here at night. It's a rite of passage in the village."

Hutter stepped onto the unnaturally flat stone. Although it was not a high perch, it gave one a more commanding feel over the river. There was peace in the slow current. In the distance, Hutter spied men fishing from the shore, bulking up a feast that would accompany the execution. A breeze moved over the black water and pressed him, carrying the familiar tang of dead fish. From here one could see where the river curled around the forest at the opposite side. On his side: the plain, the gardens, and the hovels of Strattonwick looming above. Croft stood on the ground, peering up with a hint of animosity, accusatory about something. God knew. He blocked the sun with his knobbed forearm. Rosamond had drawn attention to this deformity. Hutter tried to keep his eyes from the slick wrist.

"Are you a family man?" Croft asked.

Hutter wished the Puritan would leave him be. He'd come here to be alone, to think, to be calm after what he'd seen and heard in the forest. He left Wolfric behind, too, allowing the man space to get drunk in the quiet of the church. He understood the desire. Hutter still felt shaken. The image of Rosamond's tears turning to fleas kept him ill, soul-sick. He paced on the stone like an actor on a stage.

"A wife and two sons," he said, noncommittally. "You?" *Puritans*, he thought, *usually have large families.* He'd met Puritans with twenty children. It was sinful for a Puritan to be alone and not reproduce.

Croft took a seat on the edge of the Raven Stone. He fiddled with one of the pikes, twisting it in the loose soil. It was a morbid thing, gnarled.

"In another life," he said. He stopped there, though, and Hutter didn't care to push the matter.

"I can't imagine Strattonwick has much use for this stone," Hutter said.

"About once a generation," Croft admitted. "These pikes are dry rotted, just for show." He was silent for a moment. The breeze picked up, bending the distant garden. The stench of the river invaded one's senses. "What disturbed you out there?" he asked. "Was it because you have children? Or did she say things?"

Hutter kept pacing. He refused to look at Croft, to betray his thoughts. It occurred to him that the Puritan wanted to ask, *What did Rosamond Wise say about Israel Croft?* There was something paranoid in his manner.

"She admitted to burying the boy, as I told you."

"Did she show you things?"

Guardedly, Hutter asked, "Like what?"

It was clear that Croft battled his thoughts. He stood and began to walk away, but then he stopped.

"Witchcraft," he said, his voice barely audible in the wind. There was something desperate in his tone, as if, in his life, he'd seen the princes of Hell and genuinely feared their intrusion into this matter.

"She's just a frightened girl," Hutter said. "As well she should be." He simply couldn't bring himself to form words about what he'd seen. It was absurd. It couldn't be spoken.

Although Hutter's reply was not an answer, Croft didn't push.

"At dusk," he said, "we'll begin the feast. I want the deed done with now, not tomorrow. Are you willing?"

Hutter nodded, relieved. He dreaded another night of waiting. *They were with you in the church,* Rosamond had taunted.

"We'll be ready," Hutter said.

Croft began a trek towards the gardens where young men toiled, leaving Hutter alone on the Raven Stone. The old man moved so oddly, so disjointedly.

She said you weren't a soldier, Hutter thought, but then he reminded himself that Croft never claimed to be. *She was in my mind. Not yours.* Hutter turned to the river. *What disturbed you, Puritan?* he thought.

There was once a woodsman....

Hutter opened the door of the church and stepped into the shade. A heat haze filled the air. The air was stagnant and smelled of sweat.

"Wolf?" he called, scanning the pews. "The Puritan wants it done today." *Thank God for it,* he thought.

He moved up the aisle to the altar, where there stood a simple wooden cross, unpainted and austere with splinters. The cross was the only ornamentation in the entire building. From the front of the room, he looked about for Wolfric, but there was no sign of the man. The church was silent, save for Hutter's breathing. He walked again towards the rectangle of sunlight at the open door, checking on the floor for an unconscious, drunken Wolfric. There was no sign he'd been here at all. Their satchels remained undisturbed in the Harlot Pews.

Outside, Hutter saw a youth watching him. He waved the boy over, but the child, taught to be ashamed of speaking to such a man, ducked his head and turned away. Perturbed, Hutter followed.

"Boy," he said. "Just a question for you."

The child, no more than ten, with a moon face and unkempt red hair, halted. He kept his back turned.

Hutter spoke to him without looking in his eyes. "Have you seen the man I travel with? The large man with a blond beard."

The boy nodded.

A woman, stout and crusted with filth, hurried towards the boy. Without looking at Hutter, she took the child's hand.

"Don't speak to him," she said. "You'll soil all of us."

"Where'd you see him?" Hutter asked, trying to keep his temper down in the face of such an insult.

"He went to the forest," the child called. The woman smacked the boy's face, hard. The child let out a cry, but, with the rise of his mother's open hand, he stopped and lowered his head. The pair moved on.

Hutter stood alone, a waft of smoke obscuring his vision. *The forest?* he thought. *Not even Wolf would be such a fool as that.* Hutter started towards the trail at the rear of Strattonwick, the trail that led to Lord Allingham, the trail that led to the spot where Rosamond had called him sire of the hatchet. In haste, he cut through a pit of mud between two hovels. The muck nearly ripped off his boots.

The child had not been lying. Indeed, there sat Wolfric, on the incline where the trail began, his back to the shed that housed Rosamond, his arms draped over his knees. The guard with the cudgel was nowhere in sight. Hutter approached. Wolfric didn't seem drunk; his gaze was too aware, too inward.

"What are you doing?" Hutter asked.

"Waiting on you," he said. Gone was the vivacious tone, the vitriol. Wolfric spoke flatly, as a man traumatized. "I have something to show you."

"The Puritan wants it done today," Hutter said. "I thought that would please you. Is the girl in there?"

Wolfric shrugged. "You're not listening to me. I want to show you something."

"What is it?" He noticed now that dry mud caked Wolfric's hands.

Wolfric stood. There was no evidence he had had anything to drink. He was too steady.

"Follow me," he said. "Those things aren't here. At least they're hiding themselves better now. It isn't far."

"Who's guarding the girl?"

"After what you saw, that isn't a sensible question. She chooses to stay."

Hutter could not argue with that.

Wolfric led Hutter past the oasis where they had interrogated Rosamond. For Hutter, there was still a residue in the air here. The feeling moved beneath his skin. He turned his gaze from the oily surface of the pond. The trail forked. To one side, the path led onward, deeper into the forest. To the other side, the path opened into a fenced clearing, a cemetery with simple wooden crosses. Wolfric looked at his hands.

"It was the only fresh grave," he said.

"What have you done?" Such an abomination shook Hutter to the core. His anger swelled.

"I had to see," Wolfric said. He would not be intimated. The larger of the two, he reached out and gripped Hutter's arm. "*You* have to see."

Hutter struggled to free his arm but couldn't break Wolfric's iron clutch. He stopped short of striking his assistant, but his anger remained high. Wolfric pulled him through the graves and crosses, stamping with disrespect over the bodies in the earth. The grave was at the back corner beneath the fence, a mark of the unbaptized. Wolfric had not replaced the dirt in the infant's grave. Earth and stone remained piled at the side.

A stained shroud covered what lay at the bottom of the hole.

"It's very real," Wolfric said. He released Hutter's arm. "She did not lie to you."

"I didn't ask for proof," Hutter said.

"Here. Look." Wolfric knelt and pulled back the hardened shroud. A faint trace of moss had begun to grow over the cloth. "There's no smell," Wolfric said. "No rot. Just the smell of the dirt."

Of the mound, Hutter thought. *Almost pleasant.*

Although a black, peeling layer of skin covered the skull and erupted in swaths over the body, there were other areas of the child exposed. Rather than bones, tree roots formed a skeleton beneath the flesh. It occurred to Hutter that the infant had been growing flesh, and that the process was incomplete. The child had no nose and no more than a lanced boil for a mouth.

Wolfric touched one of the legs. "Light as kindling," he marveled. "Just sticks. Like a doll."

There was another presence in their midst. Hutter started. His heart was hard against his chest. He turned, expecting the Puritan to be standing among the crosses. It was not Israel Croft whom he saw, but Rosamond Wise. She gripped a hatchet, not unlike the one Hutter wore, and there was blood up her arm. The blood, he could see, was her blood. There was a wound on her forearm as wide and wet as an open mouth. Mites scuttled from the gash.

"You see now?" she asked.

Hutter wanted to turn away, but the woman's approach mesmerized him. He couldn't look away. Wolfric, still on his knees, his mind battered, wept.

Rosamond handed the hatchet to the executioner. She did so with calmness. She placed her wounded arm on the fence. "Take one of the fingers," she said. "Sire of the hatchet," she purred. "Cutter of the cross."

"Why do you call me that?"

"There once was a woodsman," she started, as if she were telling a story to a child, but she left the thought unfinished. "Once a woodsman here."

Hutter, delirious, gripped the hatchet. As instructed, he brought down the blade against one of her fingers. When the blow was done, the finger severed, Rosamond recoiled in pain. Tears rimmed her eyes, each turning into a flea and bounding forth into the woods. She did not cry out, although she felt agony as anyone would feel it.

Wolfric picked the finger from the pile of grave dirt. He wiped the blood on his shirt.

"No bone," he marveled. He wiped tears from his face. "Just a piece of the root."

Madness, Hutter thought, yet he looked. Indeed, the still warm flesh encased a dark, splintering root. His stomach grew sick, his head light.

"Leave us," Rosamond said. Her hand, although she gripped it tightly, bled profusely. Her face was ghastly white, her thin lips colorless.

Hutter helped Wolfric from the ground. The assistant, he noticed, placed the severed finger in his pocket. Rosamond did not object. What could be hidden now? As the two men, absorbed and silent, moved through the graves, Rosamond went to her knees. She swept dirt into the child's grave with her undamaged hand. Now she was weeping, too.

In the boughs of a sprawling tree, Hutter saw the skeletal movements of other infants, moving with the deftness of felines. With the knots of their eyes, he presumed, they watched, but they did not interfere.

Who, here, knows their mother?

A crowd gathered by the river in Strattonwick, but there was no feast. Tables had not been brought forth. There were no fire pits to prepare the fish or roast the vegetables. The sun was at its pinnacle, and the day was hot. No one spoke or bustled for space. Tension laced the air. The men, women, and children, poor, dirt-caked peasants, God-fearing, demon-haunted, simply stood and looked on at the Raven Stone in wonder, as they would've done if Jesus Christ lowered from the clouds. There were nearly forty villagers. The river behind the stone moved slowly, unchanged. The sun shone over the oily water. The boat that would have been used for drowning Rosamond Wise waited against the shore, punched into the mud. There was a large and empty burlap sack in the vessel. There was a pole to ensure the drowning. None of these things drew the attention of the villagers. It was the grisly vision upon the Raven Stone that arrested their minds. The sight would either turn the villagers pious or lead them to debauchery. Time would tell.

The blood seemed like nothing to them. Other, more personal, details brought them horror.

Hutter and Wolfric, emerging from the forest, trudging through lines of hovels, passing through the gardens, caused no disturbance in this gathering by the river's edge. Their presence went unheeded. Nor did the executioner and his assistant speak to one another once the sight was clear. What was there to say? What could ever be said? There would only be the images, sights like this.

The villagers, and now Hutter and Wolfric, gazed in awe upon the work of Rosamond's hatchet.

Master Israel Croft, his Puritan shield of brown cloth removed, his flesh splayed, razored open, lay across the stone in a pool of blood. How the girl had overpowered him, or even caught the old man by surprise, was unclear. Maybe the roots in the forest did more than watch and stalk. The Puritan's head had been severed, cut without precision from his shoulders. Where the skin had been removed from his body, where bones should have protruded, there was a system of roots. The sinew at his neck looked like vines, the meat like wet moss.

He, too, Hutter thought, awed. *Who, here, knows their mother? Who else has severed a piece of their body to learn their heritage?*

The great drama of Strattonwick had played out between Croft and Rosamond: the one who embraced the truth and the one who denied it. How many others with similar dilemmas of thought existed here?

Wolfric, dazed, retrieved Rosamond's finger from his pocket. He examined the digit closely, like a Catholic with his relic, preferring it to the sight of Croft. It told the same story, after all.

Hutter wondered if his companion would ever regain his mind. "There's nothing for us here," Hutter whispered. He took Wolfric by the arm and tried to lead him, but the man was too stubborn, too strong. He separated from Hutter's grasp and melted into the crowd of villagers.

Hutter looked to the forest road, so near, and felt dread. The road passed the mound, the mother's belly. He would have to look upon the knoll once more, and he'd have to do so with nothing more than a hatchet. He started away, leaving Wolfric behind. He hoped the man, his friend, would regain himself and follow, but he could not wait for the transformation. He had to rely on his own strength, his own cunning now. The journey was very long. Even the journey to the Channel was long. As he moved from the crowd towards the gardens, something he'd said to Wolfric upon their arrival here returned to him, and the irony of it struck like a hammer.

We'll be leaving the richer, he'd told his companion.

God loathes hubris, Hutter thought.

GRIMOIRE *of the*
FOUR IMPOSTORS.

AN
ENCOUNTER
in 1724

Before a venerable gathering of the Royal Society of London, Dr. Béla Toth closed his lecture with an appeal. He had been speaking for almost an hour. Generous fireplaces burned on each side of the hall, bringing the heat of the confined room to an intolerable level. Each minute seemed to make the room warmer. Toth felt the weight of his audience gathering against him but, rather than folding to pressure, he pushed back. In such an emotional state, he failed to mask his accent. It was the Hungarian tones of his father, disturbingly foreign to the English. It was an accent capable of anger, passion, and desperation simultaneously. Toth had always worked diligently to conceal his true manner of speaking, in his time in Ireland and in his time here, managing (although never successfully erasing) inflections and vowels with care, but now he spoke without effort to conceal.

An appeal to the intellect had once again failed. A catalogue of evidence was not enough. He decided to appeal to emotion. He had nothing to lose. Toth stripped away the eldritch jargon of his craft and spoke simply and emphatically. Any Puritan in the audience had leached from the crowd, leaving early in the talk. The remaining men, he hoped, were men he could sway—men open to the ideals of an occultist. Pansophism—the search for all knowledge, even that which was hidden—was the term once, a century prior. Toth was a dignified man of noble lineage, his father a man of enormous wealth and influence a world away, but the courtier's nonchalance disappeared as he spoke with fevered gesticulations. He planted his fist against the podium. The rattle went through the crowd. His face reddened.

A robed man in a wig of dark curls, a headpiece that mimicked poorly the style of the Bourbons, stood and left the room. Hints of lavender moved in clouds as he walked. Another man followed. The door slammed in their wake. The fires that burned in the twin hearths on either side of the room trembled from the breath of air through the door. Toth paused, watching, vexed. A shadow moved over the podium as another man, a rotund Fellow in brown, stood. Once this man departed, less than ten remained in the room. Politeness kept them anchored. Dr. Toth saw little curiosity in the smudge of shadowed faces.

The thought occurred to him that he was leaping a great chasm. He had run with all his might and jumped. The reflective thought could not be chased away once it entered his mind. The image, the futility of it, sapped his will. Now, in the middle of that leap, he felt as though he had miscalculated, and that the opposite ledge was much farther away. Despite effort, he'd fall. The momentum of his appeal slowed. Pulling back from the podium, he said, somewhat defensively, "Searching the occult is not akin to a rat hunting in plague pits. One of your men has said that. He is wrong. We mustn't destroy knowledge that has come before us. That was the folly of the Dark Ages. Consider the sources you neglect. Think of your John Dee. Why is he dismissed only two centuries after Elizabeth admired him? Why is Michele Nostradamus forgotten? What of Paracelsus?" Toth's voice was like a whisper now. The final question went unheard, he assumed.

It was a breathless but impotent entreaty. He aborted his lecture then, allowing the final question to hang in the air. The din of the fires, crackling logs, replaced his words. The Fellows did not applaud. They did not even murmur. Toth had expected a slew of questions, both curious and angry, but he looked upon a sea of bemused faces. The man who stood before them was a foreigner in speech, but he was also a foreigner in thought. Here was no empiricist, that much was clear, and empiricism was the flavor of the day. Mentally, the Society's Fellows consumed Toth and regurgitated him. There were no questions, which was the greatest of insults with a crowd such as this. The men stood and departed to a study in which only Royal Fellows were permitted. One after another the men exited through the door. It was a patient action, bored, typical of any uneventful night in this hall. When the men had gone, only the secretary, Henry Birch, and a young man whom Toth did not know remained behind.

Birch, wearing a coat of black velvet and a lace ruff, thanked Dr. Toth for addressing the Society. He was a distracted man, his words in one hand and his mind in the other. He assured Toth that his remarks would be included in the next edition of the *Philosophical Transactions*. The promise was almost lurid. Judging from Birch's tone, Toth hoped his remarks would not appear in the journal. He would be lampooned.

Then, unceremoniously, Birch said, "Master Thomas will show you the door, Dr. Toth. God bless, and good evening to you." At that, the secretary turned and departed. As he cracked open the door to the side chamber, faint laughter emerged.

Toth had failed then. He felt very alone. He was not invited to sit and speak with the Fellows of the Royal Society, to drink brandy and exchange pleasantries. *In the chamber of job offers,* he thought, *of pacts and promises of goodwill.*

Thomas Fretwell introduced himself. A man of no more than twenty, he gave a slight bow and motioned towards the door at the rear of the lecture hall—the door through which the Puritans had first exited. "This way, Dr. Toth," he said.

Toth gathered his notes and removed the folio of manuscripts from the podium. He lifted his overcoat. He felt drained to the point of being ill. Dejected, he thought, *this was a last chance.* He could not return to a post at Trinity College—he'd been ostracized for good this time. His dismissal was permanent. His teaching post, in fact, no longer existed—it was too old-fashioned to replace, he'd been told. Admittedly, the Royal Society had been kinder in rejection than his committee for tenure at Trinity, but he wouldn't find a career in London either it seemed, not via the Society anyhow. He'd truly believed his learning would find an audience in such a progressive city, with such an august gathering of open-minded men. What did these men have to fear from the occult? Such an idea was provincial. It belonged in Ireland or Hungary, perhaps, but not here. Of course, this was wrong. Every place was provincial in its own way. Any fool could see that.

Toth was sweating rather heavily, he realized. He took a handkerchief from his pocket and dabbed at his face. The room was like Hell. He couldn't fathom why such a small space needed two fires.

Fretwell watched him patiently. He had a different look in his eyes than the others. Sympathy, perhaps.

"Why did those men not leave?" Toth asked Fretwell. He pointed at the side chamber. "Why didn't they depart with the Puritans?"

Fretwell did not answer this. Toth, as often happened when he was in close proximity to another, especially one sympathetic, teased a stray thought from the young man's mind. Having a special and rare ability, he had developed his own idea of ethics about such things. He looked at the intrusion as others looked at overhearing a conversation. Thoughts were there to be grabbed. Fretwell's idea was jumbled, difficult to decipher, but a familiar expression of ridicule lay somewhere inside of it. Curiously, it was ridicule of Puritan men rather than ridicule of Toth or his occultism. That much was pleasing.

Toth drew his own conclusion. "They wanted fodder. Just like Birch for the *Transactions*. And you?" he asked bitterly.

Fretwell led Toth into the outer corridor, which was empty of people. There were five candles against each wall and myriad portraits of famous men and noblemen stared down from the heights. Toth's footsteps were loud against the tiled floor. The Royal Society now seemed a very lonely place, forlorn to one locked out of the inner chambers. Fretwell said nothing until they had reached the antechamber that held the front entrance. A portrait of Charles II hung above the doorway. A chandelier descended from the ceiling, a simple but expensive decoration. Winter pressed against the heavy door. Wind with an edge of ice breathed through the fissures. Distant from a hearth, the hall was damp, cold, and shadowed.

"I'm no Fellow of the Society," Fretwell said. "I'm only a student. I came to hear you speak, although I feel you won't believe that."

Toth studied the man's face. He was a tremendously pale young man, as if childhood sickness had left him bloodless. His hair and his eyes were pale. Toth wondered if the man had even seen a summer. He had dark rings around his eyes. "Where do you attend school?" he asked.

"Cambridge."

"Cambridge, sir, and you're interested in the occult? How come they haven't thrown you in Bedlam?"

Without pretense, and ignoring the last remark, Fretwell nodded. "Very much so, sir. I study natural philosophy at the university, but I would've been an occultist like you a century ago."

"There's the rub, is it not? A century ago." Toth shook his head. "How do Cambridge boys get in here?"

"Dr. Isaac Newton attends irregularly. If you're an acquaintance of Professor Newton, and you desire to hear the lecturers, you get to perform menial tasks here at the Society. Free labor from the curious. Tonight I get to show the lecturer to the door in return for taking the professor's place." Fretwell smiled. He was a somewhat soft young man—a little cloistered, a little anxious, a little naïve. Yet, Thomas Fretwell knew what he was about. There was genuine confidence beneath this exterior.

"I see," Toth said as a way of goodbye. "I have a great deal to consider tonight, Master Fretwell. Good evening—"

"—May I speak freely to you, Dr. Toth?" Fretwell narrowed his eyes, checking down the corridor. Still, they were alone.

"If done quickly, yes."

Before continuing, Fretwell hesitated, as if confronting a shade of doubt. No, Toth realized, he had stalled intentionally. He had looked inward and felt Toth rummaging through his mind. Fretwell asked, "You're trying to see what I'm thinking, aren't you, Dr. Toth?"

Jarred, Toth said, "You gave no indication." He hesitated now, wondered how much he should say, if he should say anything at all. There were those who believed the ability to be diabolic in origin. "You can feel it?" He was astounded. The childish question was all he could muster.

"We're of kindred minds," Fretwell said. "I certainly didn't indicate such a thing. Look at how these men treated you." He opened the door then. "As you said, the Cambridge elders would have me tossed into Bedlam." The busy night rushed inward. "Come outside."

Lit by two lanterns glowing over the front entrance, the cobbled street in front of the Royal Society was shadowy. Ice had begun to meld the stones into an unbroken sheet. London never slept, not even when the weather was treacherous. A horse and carriage and bundled driver approached. The man passed by without a glance. The wheels reverberated against the surrounding wood and stone. Tall buildings lined the labyrinthine streets.

Toth and Fretwell descended a short flight of steps. A light snow fell now, coating the ground. When Fretwell pointed east, white flakes spotted his sleeve. "On nights like this you can still smell where the city burned," he said. "Even after six decades."

He's an empath, too, Toth thought. He breathed in until the city filled his lungs. Indeed, the aroma of charred wood moved on the wind, a phantom residue. Winter teased the smell from the marrow of London, at least for one with the ability to catch it.

"To be truthful, I traveled here to meet you and hear you speak for one reason," Fretwell said. He crossed his arms in defense against the winter. His breath was a cloud of frost, obscuring his eyes. His lily whiteness stood in marked contrast to the Roma-blooded Hungarian. "I need to consult with you about a witch and a book," he said. "A grimoire."

Shock must have registered on Toth's face. He could not have hidden the feeling as it pinched his mind to a singular point. He became foolish with questions. "The Nottingham woman?" Toth asked. "How many know of this book?"

Fretwell said, "She told me to come to you. She told me of no other." He wrung his gloveless hands, white as bones. His coat was thin and his clothes poor. He wore a dark scarf of no value. He was a rather pitiful sight, like a knight with a title and no money. Toth wondered at this. Fretwell did not belong at the Royal Society any more than he. His origins were humble, indeed. At this moment, both could well be subjects of ridicule on the tongues of the Fellows.

"You've seen her too, then," Fretwell said. He seemed more relieved than disturbed. He was looking at the reflection of sanity. "Thank God," he muttered.

"She's haunted me since I left Dublin," Toth admitted. He regretted saying this. He cursed himself. His face burned red.

"What troubles you?" Fretwell asked.

"I won't talk of it tonight," Toth said. "I can't."

"Tomorrow then?" Fretwell asked.

Toth turned and walked away. Although it was a long and harrowing walk to take, he had to be alone. He had to think. Such talk, if overheard, could warrant arrest. Even as an occultist, he had to keep distant from the label of witchcraft.

"Where are you staying?" Fretwell called after him. "We can talk of it tomorrow."

Toth shook his head. He said nothing. *I can't be drawn into this*, he thought.

Fretwell cursed, but he didn't follow.

Dr. Toth placed a candle on the table at the side of his bed. A halo of soft light spread across the room and up the nearest wall. The room, for which he'd paid little, held a bed, a table, a washbasin on the table, and water-stained (this was an optimistic thought) walls. With the shutters outside the window busted and broken, and the shutters on the inside of the room completely missing, a thick rime covered the pane. The glass frosted inside and out, making the window opaque as crystal. Wind rattled the frame and lanced the gaps. The bed was a hard straw mattress suspended on a weave of sagging ropes. With any weight, the mattress grazed the abominably dirty floor. When the room was in full darkness, mice congregated beneath the bed, emerging from under the floorboards and from within the walls.

There was nothing fine about the room or the inn that housed it. For that matter, there was nothing fine about the street and borough that housed the inn. Rowdy voices from the street below pierced the walls, a constant occurrence throughout the night. Drunken men, exiting the first floor tavern, guffawed and sang at odd hours. Feet trampled the floorboards above his room. A woman giggled. She had been with several men already tonight, and giggling was her usual opening to the exchange of wares. Traffic didn't cease in the halls outside his door until long past midnight. Abysmally, Toth couldn't help but to compare this life to the one he'd led at Trinity. He felt the descent keenly.

The room had no hearth, so Toth wore several layers of clothes and a sleeping cap to keep his ears warm. His hands were hard and red. He took a seat on the mattress. After placing a large leather folio on the soiled sheet, he maneuvered the candle, merely a stub now, to better light the manuscripts within. He had stopped short of bringing forth this collection of grimoires to the Fellows of the Royal Society. Displaying the books, waxing romantically about their contents, would have only invited derision, he'd concluded. He'd been poised, of course, to bring out one of the books, to show the men that a grimoire was, although exceptional in content, mundane in appearance. Flesh did not bind these books, as zealots often claimed. Blood did not serve as their ink. Poised, yes, but the mood was never right. Therefore, he'd kept the lecture in the abstract. He wondered now if that had been the right decision.

What invaluable books, though, he mused, admiring the array. He separated the manuscripts from the folio. He had brought five exemplary books along for this journey, leaving the remainder of his collection in Dublin. Here were some of the more obscure texts he'd collected during his years at Trinity, either through his own searching or via his uncle, Dorin Toth, once a professor in Vienna. *The Marriage of Nine Tails*, for instance, which he'd discovered hidden in a larger work by Agrippa in a Muscovy library of law. It was an extraordinary work. He knew of few others that lifted the veil so exquisitely. *The Marriage of Nine Tails* took healing as its subject, but it would never be a book recognized by a man of medicine. Once, perhaps, but not now, not in this mechanical age.

Another: *The Enochian Alchemy* was a secret work by John Dee, the Queen's philosopher. This was a dangerous book, one of the few Toth would label as such. Something quite dark found illumination herein. There were no angels in this book, unlike the majority of Dee's work in occultism. The thin pamphlet was of incalculable value, priceless. A man could properly ruin his soul with *The Enochian Alchemy*. The first hours after death constituted its subject. What would men pay to know such things? A fortune, they'd claim, and yet the same men would ignore the knowledge when it was before them.

Toth cupped his face in his hands. These five books alone represented what the occult could add to the store of man's knowledge. Each handwritten text was the only copy of its kind. Hundreds of such books existed in the world, many of them buried or lost, waiting to be rediscovered, while some were lost forever. All of the books were scorned, but there was nothing to be reviled here. The new science could never reveal the things these books revealed. The notion was as preposterous as Jesuits measuring the length of a human soul and arguing over whether the answer should be recorded in inches or digiti. Hidden knowledge could not be placed under a lens of magnification and observed thusly. There was more to the world than measuring sticks. One had to find the veil, and then one had to have the courage to lift it. These authors had moved the veil aside. Admittedly, it was unsettling to note that each, too, had concluded that the universe was malignant rather than benign, and that once in a while the malignant eye turned on Man. These books attempted to give the reader a chance to turn an eye back: the *Hieroglyphs of Ba'al*, in particular.

Without gin or sleep, Toth's mind was manic. He stood and began to pace the room, moving from the frosted window to the door. His thoughts turned to Thomas Fretwell, the one member of the audience tonight who wouldn't have scoffed at the display of manuscripts. The young man, as he himself had claimed, was of a kindred mind. A man didn't meet many of his own spirit in the world.

Toth, more distant from his failed lecture at the Society, regretted not confessing more to Fretwell. The man had been compelled to spill his heart out. He had, practically, and Toth almost reciprocated. He nearly told of how the Nottingham woman, regardless of her various tactics, professed a single entreaty:

Irretrievably, the book will be lost. The destruction of it will be permanent.

Since sailing across from Ireland, the crone had been a recurring presence in Toth's dreams. She showed him what a zealous magistrate did to her in Nottingham. She showed him caves under the city where waifs gathered and huddled over fires. Toth saw vivid images of the witch's hanging body, the hem of her dress tied shut to prevent gawking, her corpse freezing in the snow, swaying in the wind. The way she moved, she resembled the broken limb of a tree.

Behind all the images, she spoke repeatedly of the book. The *Grimoire of the Four Impostors*, she called it, although Toth had never known of such a text. His ignorance did nothing to invalidate the existence. No one, no matter how immersed in the subject, knew of all grimoires. Their nature precluded such a possibility. The manuscript, composed in Enochian, had come to the Nottingham woman from the decaying estate of a Lady Willoughby. Prior to this, she could not say, although a vague impression of the East manifested. Its age she could not say. The grimoire, the witch claimed, revealed a power to animate, to bring impostors and imitations to life, vivify things of mimicry and bring those things into the world. This was the revelation of *Four Impostors*.

Frustrated, Toth dashed his plans of studying his texts and pinched out the candle. He pulled the sleeping cap down until it touched his eyes. A nearly complete darkness, save for the bluish coating on the window and a crease of candlelight beneath the door, blanketed the room. Toth moved aside the portfolios and positioned himself on the bed.

I'm not going to Nottingham, he thought in Hungarian. He wanted to be defiant. His eyes were not interested in the room's shadows, so he closed them and tried to force sleep. His mind stayed rampant. The inner debate raged on. *If the magistrate's men found such a book*, he reasoned, *they'd surely burn it. Why would they not pick apart her belongings? One witch to the Puritan-minded meant a nest of witches. They'd talk of black Sabbaths and covens. They'd scour the town. Her books, the mere fact that she was a literate crone, would be of chief interest to them. The book is gone.* Travelling northward to Nottingham, whether he was curious about the book or Fretwell, simply was not worth the risk. Inserting himself into such an ordeal could only bring harm. If the Puritans were zealous, as their nature insisted, he could find himself on the gallows.

What could be gained? *A great deal,* a small voice inside him said. The idea of an obscure grimoire burned in him.

I'm going back to Hungary, he countered. *I have no need to stay. I haven't seen family in a decade.* Toth had seventeen brothers and sisters.

His thoughts wandered into odder areas as he drifted closer to sleep. The diversion was merciful. Noises in the street became more intermittent as the hours passed. The floorboards above his room ceased to groan, as did the customers.

He turned on his side, his back facing the other half of the mattress and the room's doorway. Toth curled on the edge of the bed and felt the cold of the room acutely. It was then, without a sound of warning, that a foreign weight entered his bed. Toth's body shifted backward as the mattress lowered. It was physical movement rather than the sensation of a dream. The straw crackled. The ropes protested. The sheet lifted, and a large figure slid below. Toth's heart moved into his throat. It felt as though a block of ice had been placed in the bed. The acrid, familiar smell of pitch filled the air. A wave of cold pricked his flesh. Toth creased his eyes, but there was no additional light in the room. The door was not open. The window, he could see, was closed and the frost undisturbed. The world around him remained near silence—it was very late now, near morning. The figure inched closer to his back, straining the bed, and the body was ice cold.

Frozen, he thought, *like the witch swaying in the wind.*

Béla Toth closed his eyes and kept them shut. He was too frightened to look, and each moment he didn't look it became more impossible to do so. His breath he could not control, however. He breathed in uneven gasps, nearing a state of hyperventilation. Panic constricted his throat. A long finger of bone, covered in a rime thick as that on the windowpane, grazed the nape of his neck. The freeze went through him, paralyzing his nerves. A nail hard as obsidian pressed into his skin. His neck became so deeply cold it felt as though his skin would turn black from exposure.

A voice that entered his thoughts yet made no vibration in the air said, *turn and see.*

Toth refused. His heart was hard against his chest, and he wanted this to be over, but he refused. He brought his knees upward, curling into a fetal position. The command returned to him, and again he refused.

The remainder of a long hand rested against his neck, and then the hand ran into his hair, pushing the sleeping cap upward. The skin was coarse, almost jagged with ridges. Long nails pressed into his scalp. The odor of pitch, tinged with decay, became nauseating. His stomach turned sick. He felt an urge to vomit, but vomiting required movement, and, by power of will alone, he resisted. Sweat erupted over his face, despite the cold.

You'll find Fretwell at your doorstep in the morning. It was the same strained voice the Nottingham woman used in his dreams.

Transmigration, he thought, awed by her ability to compel, even in death.

You will follow him, she said. The nails pricked at his scalp.

He refused. Terror made him resolute.

Follow him or turn and see.

Still, he refused.

The hand moved to the side of his face. The flesh was hard as stone. Regrettably, he creased one of his eyes and peered. He saw the outline of the darkened fingers.

Follow him or face me.

He didn't reject the demand. He chose.

The hand retreated, scraping his cheek as it moved.

When you reach Nottingham, you'll find a boy to follow. A child. You will follow him, too. In the end, he will serve you.

A series of visions, vivid as a magic lantern show, filled Toth's mind. The remainder of the night, he later realized, fully passed in the course of this phantasmagoria.

He saw thus:

Beneath the sandstone rock of Nottingham, another city: one of caves. The tunnels and hovels were man-made. Scraped and chiseled. These were not as complex and thorough as catacombs. There were storage rooms and cellars beneath taverns. There were escape routes beneath Nottingham Castle. Towards the back of the city, when one left the shadow of the Church of St. Mary's the Virgin, a gothic cathedral, when one entered through a metal grating that looked like a door in the side of a cliff, one entered a living potter's field. A dank passage led down into the earth, and the passage opened into caves of various shapes and sizes, all hand-cut. Here the indigent lived—Nottingham's equivalent of London's street urchins. Here the witch lived in a cavern full of soot and texts. Her name was Hyacinth. She had not always been a woman of poverty.

He saw thus:

The culmination of study, the culmination of years of devotion to a single text, devotion like she had never shown anything: a deciphered code emerged. The years had brought ruin, but the secrets of the grimoire were more precious than material wealth.

He saw thus:

Hyacinth moved in the darkness where the stone was damp and cool. Droplets of water lined the ceiling. Occasionally, the water fell and formed a pool on the ground. The noise of dripping was a constant companion. She knew the way so well that she carried no candle. She carried her thoughts and nothing more. Her old body ached, bone rubbing bone where muscles had deteriorated. Walking so deeply into the caverns was no small task. Sleeping figures filled the passageways. The astringent smell of liquor coupled with that of feces and vomit grew stronger as she descended. This, she thought, was a lung of Hell.

In the deepest section of the caves, in a hole where no one had ever lived, there was a field of blood. Here the plague dead and war dead rested. Here were the victims of famine. Here were the witches and the cunning men and executed criminals. A thousand years of the dead, the oldest conjoined with the mud and rock. The last cavern was a mausoleum, a charnel house of old bones and new. Hundreds of corpses occupied the space, tucked in a pit far below the city. Bodies unfit for churchyards.

Hyacinth waded into the morass. She collected pieces that suited her needs.

He saw thus:

The careful assemblage of flesh and bone by candlelight. Mismatched bones fused together. With couplets of language, Enochian incantations gathered from the text, flesh grew like boils along the length of a femur, blossoming outward like a sprouting bud. Trembling movement followed the flesh. She regarded the first drunken pirouette as a wondrous achievement, and it was.

Quick death followed. The flesh withered. The bones became disassembled. Hyacinth created and destroyed. She returned to her hovel. She returned to the pit.

Once, and only once, the magistrate's men were in the pit, waiting for her. They had tied scarves around their faces to mask the stench. They stood in the darkness without lanterns, which must've been an ordeal for them. This was the end of things.

The corpse weight remained in the bed at Toth's side for most of the night, although it showed him no more and touched him no more. He never turned and looked. It was near dawn when the mattress lifted, the weight removed. A purple tinge touched the window. The door of his room did not open, nor did the window lift, but the figure went away. The smell of pitch, to which he was growing accustomed, left no residue. It, too, had gone.

The innkeeper, a ruffled man in a leather apron, was reluctant to pour gin so early in the morning, but this was a section of London where one could purchase vice at any time of the day. Two coins swayed the man to break his habit. Toth drank gin in the tavern until his breath was hard. His eyes had a touch of fog when he finished the last. Gin was a poor substitute for sleep, but the liquor had enough edge to brace him. Life reentered his bones, and the cold air felt more distant. Still, heavy fatigue made mud of his thoughts. He paid the innkeeper and left.

When he emerged from the inn, Toth found need for another round of bracing drinks. Thomas Fretwell, dressed in the same impoverished clothes as the night prior, stood in the street with his back against a hitching rail. Toth hadn't told the man where he was staying. The place was too notorious to admit to anyone. Here Fretwell was, though, and he'd been waiting for some time. His face was ruddy and his eyes frosted. He stared through traffic at the inn, watching the door as if he'd been instructed to do so.

Toth's appearance rewarded Fretwell's faith. At the sight of Toth walking from the inn, he moved across the street, cutting in front of a man on horseback. The man cursed the lack of caution, but Fretwell ignored him. He had one thing on his mind. When he stood before Toth, he made no greeting. He simply said, "Did she come to you? She entered my room. Physically, she—"

Toth nodded.

That was enough. Fretwell allowed the confession to die. No doubt he absorbed the memory of Toth's own experience in that moment of hesitation. Toth wondered if, unlike he, Fretwell had turned and looked at Hyacinth. He probed, yet he couldn't see past the distinct colors of the man's fear. If he had looked, then what? Was it truly Hyacinth? Was transmigration the last tendril of her effort? If so, it was a Herculean finale. Toth didn't vocalize the questions. Instead, he asked if Fretwell cared for a drink this early in the morning.

"It's still night as far as I'm concerned. I didn't sleep a minute."

Resigned, Toth asked, "We're going to Nottingham, aren't we?" Of course, the conclusion was foregone.

"I've arranged a stage from King's Cross," Fretwell said. "I did it just this morning."

"A drink then?" Toth asked.

"No time," Fretwell said.

When the young man turned and started away, Toth, as the thing in his bed demanded, followed him into the street. *The dead compel the living,* he thought. An edge of excitement coupled with his fear. Fretwell sprinted through the streets, breaking through the large crowd of a workday morning. Toth ran after him, although he was in no shape to do so. The satchel of manuscripts thudded against his ample waist. A stitch manifested in his gut. *The dead compel the living.* It was extraordinary. The thought kept him moving. The faces around him were a blur. The traffic a flash. The Puritans and Jesuits would speak of Four Horsemen in a case such as this. Toth felt loathsome toward both sects, so the idea of condemnation only spurred him.

Winter mucked the roads, slowing travel to an excruciating pace. The exhilaration Toth felt upon entering the carriage at King's Cross had died a death more tedious than exposure. After eight days of jostled and cramped quarters, the stage and its four horses crossed the River Trent at Hethbeth Bridge, beyond which the hills of Nottingham loomed. A chapel, tavern, and a few lesser homes lined the edges of the stone bridge. An array of stables with leather awnings constituted a market. Below this commotion, the river moved darkly and silently. A large chunk of ice floated with the current.

Despite the shouting peddlers, the driver did not stop on the bridge. A slowly ascending flood plain, browned by the cold, opened on the other side of the river. Here in a field below the city a gibbet stood. It was a lone structure, deliberately separate from everything else, a symbol of justice presently covered in scavenging blackbirds. Although distant from the road, only one body hung from the gallows. The withered shape wore a dress, and the hem of the dress had been tied around the ankles. A raven, its shape familiar and sleek, gripped the corpse's shoulder. The cadaver was Hyacinth. From the vision Toth had seen in his last night in London, he was confident of this. The Puritan magistrate, then, had yet to cut her down. Toth turned to Fretwell, seeing that he, too, watched through a slat in the coach door.

The stage entered Nottingham through the south gate. Guards protected the gate only when it was vital, and that was not tonight. Wolves were extinct in this part of England. This was not a town of gratuities. The gate was wide open. A stable and tavern stood immediately within the walls on either side of the road. A prosaic town, Nottingham.

Snow had held off until this final leg of the trip, with only flurries in the gray sky, which was a blessing. However, it was wet mud rather than snow that proved a relentless obstacle during the journey. Eight times during the drive northward the coach's wheels had become so obstructed in morass that the horses alone could not pull them free. The coachman, a stout peasant with a gut and thick shoulders, had the passengers aid with block and tackle each time as he, with brute strength, freed the heavy carriage. One sinkhole had been two feet deep. The driver had demonstrated this by breaking off a branch and stabbing it into the mud. At least none of the wheels had broken. There was nothing glamorous or quick or pleasing about the journey. All of the passengers were a bit hardened by the trip. The mood upon arrival was glum. The passengers had never become friendly with one another, either. The dank grayness of the city did nothing to improve moods. And now the snow was finally coming on.

The stage came to rest atop a pad of crushed stone in front of a tavern called The Fat Grape. The two front windows were yellow with firelight, while the remaining windows had already been shuttered for the night. Silhouettes moved across the front glass. Smoke curled from the chimney. The coachman disembarked with a thud, neglected his horses, and rushed inside without ceremony. The man had an odd, bowlegged gait. Toth imagined him to be a veteran of the late war. A sheathed sword (his sole defense against highwaymen, apparently) batted against the side of his knee. That was that. The coachman washed his hands of his duty. The horses sweated and steamed in the cold air. Glamour, likewise, didn't mar their lives. The shire horses, tall brutes, took turns pissing with the force of a hose against the crushed stone. Streams of urine ran downwards toward the gate.

Toth and Fretwell hopped from the coach. Each man had had ample to time to examine the other's thoughts and memories during the cramped journey. When they emerged, they did so as men who had known each other a lifetime. There were no obvious secrets between them, for better or worse. It was difficult to base a friendship on such intimacy, but boredom had lowered their inhibitions about privacy.

Currently, two of their fellow passengers, both Dutchmen with eyeglasses, shouldered past without niceties and entered the tavern. A draft of warm air escaped the door. Another passenger, an old Englishman who must've felt alone with all of the foreigners in his midst, remained in the carriage, slightly jostled by the milling horses, and fumbled with a pouch of tobacco and a pipe. He looked at no one. He hadn't looked at anyone for a week.

This section of the city stood unevenly, sloping downward toward the floodplain that separated Trent and the sandstone hills. The Fat Grape and the south gate hunkered in the shadow of castle rock and the ruins of Nottingham Castle, which rose jagged and sharp at the cliff side. The old fortress had once been a watchful eye over the city, but the civil war had been unkind to it (Charles Stuart had rallied his troops here, making it a target). The hulking structure was, by appearances, uninhabited. The walls stood, both the outer walls and those of the citadel, but fire had charred everything, rendering the walls nothing more than husks. It had been many years since a nobleman called the castle home.

The city reflected this fading prestige in other aspects. Nottingham was a town of nearly five thousand souls, most of the inhabitants clustering in the market section of the city. Their houses were not modern or fine. The town had once been wealthy from hawking alabaster figurines, but it was a ragged place now, the luster riddled. Most construction halted a century and a half prior, and the buildings were frozen in Tudor designs. When the town was not ugly it was quaint, and when it was not ugly or quaint it managed the aesthetic of ruins.

Wanting separation from the driver and fellow travelers and the God-awful coach, Toth and Fretwell walked from The Fat Grape. The street was narrow and cobbled, leading upward towards castle rock and the market near its base. The winter air possessed a sharp edge, crisp and hard. A breeze pushed bits of straw from the nearby stable into the street. In an alley where a building had burned, pigs foraged. Their familiar stench tinged the smoky air. Swine, stray dogs, and cats filled the city.

"I need a drink," Toth remarked, "but God forbid I take it with the coachman. Or the Dutchmen."

Although Fretwell was deeply nervous, he managed to smile. He'd carried a fear of Hyacinth all the way from London, and the long journey had done nothing to abate the feeling. He'd had too much time for meditation. He'd been wondering at blasphemy, worrying at it until the idea made him sick. The young man believed in Hell enough for it to scare him. He'd been dreaming of Hell, Toth knew, and it was the warped and slow decay of the brain he saw rather than Dante images. For now, though, a smile: "That old man never once looked at me," Fretwell said. He stuffed his hands in his pockets for warmth and for the business of doing something with his hands. He, too, carried a satchel on his shoulder. His supplies were more vital for the journey than manuscripts. "If he hadn't kept fiddling with the pipe I'd believe him dead."

"I preferred him to the Dutchmen," Toth said. The wind was painful, cutting. Toth winced and lowered his face as a defense. "Damned Calvinists talked about nothing except the plague in Rotterdam. By the end they had me believing there'd be a wave of pestilence arriving soon. One of them said he'd seen it in Dover and Folkestone already. He said it was coming northward, probably following stage lines."

Fretwell shrugged. "It was gibberish to me. I don't speak Dutch. You're a polyglot, aren't you? How many languages do you know, anyway?"

"I nearly studied languages," Toth said. "I know seven or eight, not all of them well. If you can learn Hungarian, you can learn any language." Mentally, he counted: *Hungarian, Romani, English, German, French, Dutch, Italian, Spanish, Romanian, Arabic, Latin, Greek, Hebrew, Enochian. Fourteen then.*

Large snowflakes began to fall. A bank of snow approached from the west like a mass of fog, bringing an early dusk over the city. The temperature dropped. Only a handful of people moved through the streets, and, in this weather, none of them were particularly respectable. Toth and Fretwell kept their heads low, but it was difficult to be inconspicuous in a provincial town. The bags on their shoulders said they were travelers. No doubt, word of the coach's arrival had already spread through networks of gossip. Eyes found them.

The two men moved past a group of waifs, huddling in yet another charred alleyway. The conflagration here was not recent. One of the children broke from his group of six and came forward into the street. The wind moved bangs across his face. He wore a soiled, little hat that didn't touch his ears. His ears and nose were hard and red. His eyes were ringed. His mouth was a shade of blue. The child walked in front of Toth and demanded money. He did not ask. He simply held out a dirt-grimed hand. The fingernails were black, all the way down to the cuticles as if his hand had been smashed. Toth fetched a penny, gave it to the boy, and asked, "Don't people like you have a place to go?"

The thought that occurred to Toth seemed to occur to Fretwell at the same time. The two shared a look. Hyacinth had said, *When you reach Nottingham, you will find a boy to follow. You will follow him, too.* She had worked efficiently thus far.

Toth's accent puzzled the boy. He didn't answer the question put to him, but, after a moment, he said, "Thank you, sir."

Toth stopped the child before he could turn back to the group in the alley. He played the hunch. "Tell me something. The body hanging in front of the city. Is that the witch?"

The child's eyes hardened a little. He looked into Toth's face and then Fretwell's. He wiped his nose and nodded.

"What can you tell us about her?"

"Old Hyacinth. She lived in the caves." The boy was no more than ten years old, but there was something mature about his demeanor and speech. Maybe life hadn't allowed him to be a child, or maybe it was something more.

Toth looked into the boy's mind. The intrusion, when the connection first linked, brought a flash of emotion most people never noticed, yet the boy flinched. It could've meant nothing more than that the boy was sensitive to such things. Toth withdrew, but he'd seen enough. The child survived like a stray cat, foraging and thieving. His mother had been a prostitute. The woman left him behind when she'd traveled north towards Yorkshire. She'd made promises to return but never made good on them. The boy was what his betters derisively called a whoreson of a hangman—the lowest of scum. The boy knew all this, and he hadn't learned any of it from his mother. His life was hard, indeed.

Toth saw something else, something of the child's character, as well. He was not honest in the strictest sense, but the boy had a code of honor. He deceived only when he felt he must. Toth knew his name and his many nicknames (the child and his companions spoke a coded language the Germans called *Rotwelsch* and English called the Thieves' Cant, and in such street talk everything and everyone had nicknames), but he asked for the information, regardless. Already exotic in his speech, he didn't want to scare the boy further.

"Roland," the boy answered.

"Like the knight of Charlemagne," Fretwell said. He was taking his own look into the child's past, it seemed. His remark meant nothing at all to the boy.

Roland, growing suspicious of this detainment, peered over his shoulder for a glimpse of his companions. He rolled the penny between his fingers. The dagger on Fretwell's belt made him tense. He kept side-eyeing the weapon. The five boys in the alley were working hard, or so they pretended, at putting a fire together. The brutal, snaking wind made the work difficult.

They'd abandon him at the first sign of trouble. Fretwell's words entered Toth's mind. Toth nodded in agreement. *Scum of the earth.*

"If I bought you food, would you tell me all you know about Old Hyacinth?" Toth asked.

Roland was a wary fly wending through a spider web. With a tight wag of his head, he declined. He held out his hand for more money, though. One of the boys in the alley watched Roland closely now. He no longer pretended to be concerned with the fire. *The leader of the band,* Toth thought. Presently, the tall, sinewy child walked over. The silhouette emerged like bas-relief, and then there was a face.

"What is all this?" he demanded, as if he were a man of authority. He was older than Roland, his voice deeper. He, too, eyed the dagger at Fretwell's waist. "Is that decoration or do you know how to use it?" he asked.

Fretwell took his hands from his pockets, but he said nothing. Tension racked him.

The tall child was brutish, with two hard lines for a chin and a mouth. His nose was broken somewhat severely, as if the deed had been achieved with a brick. He had eyes like coal shards. His Adam's apple was prominent. His hands looked like unsheathed bone.

A man and wife, both bundled in layers, moved down the street in the opposite direction. The man led a horse with a blanket on its back. Presumably, they were heading towards the south gate stables. The couple kept their eyes forward as they passed, inviting no trouble. They said nothing and acknowledged nothing.

"No harm meant," Toth said. "We're not a threat to you. What's your name?"

"My name matters nary at all," the child said. "What is it you want?"

Toth scanned the child's mind, found his name to be the ridiculously old-fashioned moniker of Ethelbert, and decided not to escalate things by resorting to humiliation. "We'll pay you for information," Toth said. "Either of you who cares to talk."

"Last man who tried to pick up Roland for information had less than Christian intentions," Ethelbert said. "You learn to be careful."

Toth caught a stray memory that surfaced in the mind of Ethelbert. He intentionally withdrew from the horror of the image. *Good Christ*, he thought, properly sickened.

"Stay with him then. We'll pay both of you. We can talk at a tavern with people in it. We'll buy you food and sit you by a fire. All you have to do is talk."

"Before we agree, what is it exactly you want to know? I don't make it a habit of ratting on my brothers," Ethelbert said.

"We want to know everything you know about Old Hyacinth. If you know the caves, we want to know where she lived, too."

Ethelbert turned towards the alley and made a flash of two signs to his fellows. It was simple as that. He made the signs, and the boys melted into the shadows. The fire was still unlit—it had been a clumsy ruse.

"Call me Bert," the child said.

"I'm Dr. Béla Toth and this is Thomas Fretwell. How about that tavern at the base of castle rock?" He peered through the snow and gathering darkness, reading the sign. "Ye Old Trip to Jerusalem?"

Bert nodded. "Only a few taverns that allow us in," he said. "That being one. The finer ones in the market won't, even when we ain't beggin'."

"Let's get inside then," Fretwell said impatiently. Something bothered him deeply, maybe something he knew that Toth missed. "We'll catch our death on a night like this," he added, as if it were the cold and not his anxiety that made him want to move.

Fretwell led the way, Toth followed, and the boys remained two steps behind. Toth half-expected the children to escape with their meager loot, but they didn't. A thin layer of snow covered the ground now. The group was the first to make footprints in the fresh snow. The yellow windows of the tavern were like beacons in the budding storm.

The tavern, either Ye Old Trip to Jerusalem or The Pilgrim (depending on whether one trusted the outer or inner signage), had been cut into the sandstone of castle rock. Nottingham Castle stood above it, atop the cliff. The door claimed an origin of 1189. Better days for the city—King Richard the Lionheart days. The façade was brick and wood and faintly Tudor, despite the claim. Inside, a tight antechamber, no wider than the shoulders of two men, opened into a large room with the stone for walls and ceiling. To the left of the room, a shadowy staircase led to an upper floor. A pall of tobacco and wood smoke, tinged with the malted aroma of beer, hung in the air. A noisy fire burned in the hearth. A rotund man holding an iron poker, and with a pipe in his mouth, kept the logs moving. Occasionally, he tossed coal into the blaze. A portrait of an old Nottingham sheriff hung above the mantel. The painting was dingy with shadow and soot. The mantel held a couple alabaster figurines of Robin Hood, complete with bow and quiver of arrows.

Most of the men inside the tavern gathered in the glow of the fire, gripping steins, talking and laughing. There were no women. The presence of Toth, Fretwell, Roland, and Bert proved to be nothing more than a minor curiosity to them. For certain, they looked (and some no doubt eavesdropped when possible), but nobody cared enough to go beyond that level of involvement. The bartender served beer to Roland and Bert without asking questions. When Toth asked where the man drew a line with children in the establishment, the bartender simply said, "No gin." Then, in what he tried to make a confidential aside, "Don't get suckered in by those boys. They'll rob you blind. You ain't the first or last to take pity on the idle sort here." Toth, with a desire to be left alone and hear no more, thanked the man for his advice and paid him generously.

The four sat at a small wooden table in a corner of the pub. Splinters and knife carvings marred the planks. Shadows played over their faces. One could hear wind near the front entrance, but nothing came through the stone. The warmth of the fire went through Toth, bringing a sense of touch back into his hands. He removed his deerskin gloves. Slowly, his limbs thawed. After some time had passed, he even stripped his heavy cloak. Toth drank gin, while the three others had steins of beer. The boys ate rabidly from a plate of bread and cheese. They drank the beer with relish. It was a pitiful sight. The children didn't seem dangerous when detached from the alley shadows. They were just hard luck cases, scavengers.

Toth spoke to Bert first, because he sensed Bert needed to be shown that kind of respect. Roland had to be treated as the inferior of the two. He nodded at the food and beer. "That's our end of the deal," Toth said. "Now yours."

"Ask," Bert said, chewing. He took a drink.

"I thought your kind stayed in the caves when the weather turned. With the snow coming on, why not take refuge there? Why risk your death?"

"Ain't our desire to be in the caves," Bert said.

"Then it is a choice." Toth looked at Roland. "And you? Why not?"

Roland considered this a moment, and then he said, somewhat cryptically, "Ain't really a choice either, is it?" With a gulp, he finished the beer.

"More beer?"

Bert nodded.

Fretwell stood, moved through the crowd, and fetched three more beers. Bert's eyes were swimming after a few dips into the second stein. Tough or not, he hadn't the weight.

"Why isn't it a choice?" Toth asked.

Bert tried to shake lucidity back into his head. His eyes were there and not there. He deferred to Roland.

Roland said, looking over the tall stein, "Hyacinth. What else?"

Toth took a sip of gin. The fire warmed him from the outside and the alcohol from within. "She was executed. We saw her hanging by the river."

"She left enough behind," Roland said.

"Like what?"

Bert shrugged and cut in. "Ain't really sure, to be honest. And that's the God's honest. Just somethin' in the caves. You try to sleep down there, and you'll feel it, too."

Roland agreed.

Bert went on. "Ever since she died it's been like that. The caves turned us all off one by one. It wasn't even something we talked about. Some of the older boys got inside the old castle. It's a little Hell-den up there when night falls. You can buy anything you fancy. Magistrate will have the place torn down stone by stone come spring. I imagine he'd like to have us all drowned in the river while he's at it."

"There isn't anybody staying down in the caves now?"

"Ain't but a handful of folks livin' there. Most of them are staying in the cellar under St. Mary's. That cave ain't connected to anything except the church. Those are the real old folks who can't work. That's about it. Rest is turned out into the streets."

"Under St. Mary's is haunted, too," Roland added. He pushed his beer aside. "She haunts it, connected to the main shafts or not."

"She does," Bert agreed.

Fretwell pulled out a bag of coins. It was a small purse that he kept inside his coat. "What would it take for you two to lead us down there?"

"Why would you want to do that?" Bert asked.

"We're looking for a book Hyacinth owned," Toth said. "A book called *Grimoire of the Four Impostors*. It'd be a handwritten book, not printed."

"I wouldn't tell that to the magistrate," Bert said. "He'd take you as a witch, too. I've heard he's got the fever for it."

"Are you a witch?" Roland asked. "Sometimes folk traveled here to see Hyacinth, when she was living, I mean, and I guess they were witches themselves." Roland had a knowing look, as if he had suspected an admission of sorcery since feeling Toth enter his thoughts.

"Necromancers came to see her, the way I heard it," Bert said.

"Nothing of the sort. Rare book dealers," Toth lied. "Up from London."

Bert scoffed. He was irreverent to begin with, but, when drunk, he was a true heathen. "Yeah, you sound like it, mate. Where are you from really?"

"Hungary. It's far in the east, north of Greece."

Of course, this meant nothing to Bert or Roland. They knew little beyond the English Channel. They nodded, though, as if it did.

"You'll have a tough time finding anything that belonged to Hyacinth," Bert said. "Magistrate had his men down in the caves searching. They ran everyone out of that section and made a burn pile after she was hanged."

"I bet, by God, if they knew it was worth something they wouldn't burn it," Roland said. "Greedy bastards, they are. Each of them. The magistrate more than the rest. He wears a wig down to his waist. Puritans don't often wear wigs, but he does. You can't miss him. He has a French wife. I think he paid quite a bit for her."

"I sure as Hell would," Bert added.

Roland smiled and took a drink.

Bert eyed Toth. "We're talking shillings, not pennies if you want us to take you down there."

"That's fine. It's urgent, though. It has to be tonight."

The boy smirked a little. "And that ain't to say we'll be staying down there with you, neither."

"I didn't imagine you'd ever admit to being afraid," Fretwell said. He'd finished his second beer now. He pushed the stein away so as not to obscure his face or his meaning.

Bert breathed through his mouth. "Around certain folks I wouldn't dare it. I don't give half a damn what a fop like you thinks, though. See, I'm starting to get the idea that that dagger *is* just decoration. You're too soft to use it, I'd guess. Maybe it was a gift from your mum."

Toth shook his head and eyed Fretwell. *Enough*, he projected. *Stop antagonizing him.*

He may not be the one.

He may not.

I get a feeling he'll lock us down there, Fretwell countered.

Not if you pay him enough.

In the silence, Bert finished his beer. He swapped steins with Roland and worked on what was left there.

"What was Hyacinth like?" Toth asked.

"I never had any dealings with her," Bert said curtly. He watched Fretwell as he spoke. His face had reddened.

"I did," Roland said.

"You didn't," Bert retorted. He took another drink. He was getting sloppy now. Beer ran down his chin.

Roland nodded, perfectly sober. "My mother went to her once to wash a child out of her belly. Hyacinth made a tonic for that sort of thing. I was told she tried to wash me out like that. I saw Hyacinth out by the Trent once, and I asked her about it. This was a couple years back."

"What'd she say to you?" Toth asked.

"She didn't say anything. She just stared at me a moment, like she was sizing me up."

She could see his thoughts, Toth projected.

Fretwell nodded heavily.

"She did that a second, and then she turned and took her pail and went off. She had a presence about her like she was somebody important."

"That's the only time?" Toth asked.

"That's it. Everybody talked about her being an ugly old crone. She wasn't ugly, though, not when you looked at her close. I'd even guess she was pretty when she was young. She was old and that's about all. She wasn't a bit ugly."

"Two shillings a piece," Fretwell offered. He put the money on the table.

Bert wasn't impressed. He made a dismissive gesture. "Double it," he said.

Fretwell grimaced. His face grew red, too, now. "Fine. Four shillings a piece."

"Let's see 'em."

Fretwell placed the coins on the table. He pushed the array across.

Roland whistled.

"I said we're not staying down there with you," Bert said. "I wanna make that very clear."

"How much would that take?" Fretwell asked.

"Oh, you could buy me this tavern for starters," Bert said. He smirked again. "And you could hand over that toy dagger. I wouldn't want it to scratch your lady hands by accident."

Toth touched Fretwell's arm before the young man could snap back. *Enough,* he thought.

Bert kept laughing until the rotund man at the hearth pointed the iron poker at him and then at the door.

Toth nodded. He rose to leave.

The streets of Nottingham were dark now, covered in a layer of snow that glistened when lanterns were near. Snow continued to fall, piling on rooftops. Fires, ringed by freezing urchins, burned in a few empty lots and alleys.

As the four passed a particularly large group of homeless, Bert said, "You can see what I mean." Men, women, children, and stray dogs huddled among the group. "The caves are turning them out."

Toth nodded. With anticipation building, his nerves burned. Over the crunching footfalls, he asked, "There haven't been others in the city inquiring about Hyacinth?"

"Not that I've heard," Bert said. "And I'd hear. Wait and I'll get you a torch from that fire."

Fretwell fetched a small metal lantern and candle from his satchel. He handed the material over to Bert. The lanky child moved towards the group. He did little to acknowledge the greeting he received. He grunted at the multitude of questions about the strangers. He lit the candle and secured the lantern.

She'll protect us, Toth thought. *She called us here for a purpose.*

I saw what she was constructing, Fretwell returned. *As did you.*

Toth said nothing.

It's not her ghost they're worried about.

Bert returned with the light, which he handed off to Fretwell.

Toth's heightened nerves became dread when Bert and Roland moved past St. Mary's Church of the Virgin towards a protruding cliff of rock. He had seen this in his vision. It was surreal to walk a path his mind had already travelled. The face of the rock was sheer, straight up and down. Chiseled graffiti, a few symbols Toth recognized as Enochian, and a metal grating marred the wall of stone. The hole beyond the grating was black. Pieces of snow blew through the grillage and disappeared. The gate was ajar, unlocked. The metal bars trembled when wind cut through, which made the grillage too busy to hold snow.

"You've been through it more," Bert said to Roland. "Tell 'em the lay."

Roland breathed warmth into his hands. "That passageway has enough caverns to put the town inside it. Hyacinth's is the one with ashes piled inside. The magistrate did that. You might find everything burned or you might not. You keep going and you'll end up in a grave pit that nearly comes even with the river bottom. There's a thousand or more dead in there. You get through that and you're out again, but down in the meadow by Trent. You get out of that passage and you'll see the gibbet pretty near."

"She'll be waitin' on you," Bert said, laughing. "Frozen solid, too."

"That isn't enough," Fretwell said. "We paid you to show us, not tell us."

"I ain't goin' in there," Bert said. "Besides, you already paid up."

"You're a damned heathen, you know that?" Fretwell snapped.

Bert's eyes narrowed. He reached inside his coat and pulled a dagger of his own. The blade was nicked and beaten. "Let's see how you do with that toy of yours," he said. "I've been waitin' for this."

Fretwell straightened.

"Enough," Toth demanded. "Get on your way and leave us be."

Bert smirked. "Hand over what's left in the purse, and I'll do just that. I won't even run to the magistrate and tell him about your book. I won't tell him a damn thing about you."

Roland cut in. "Stop playing it so hard. Back off." Then, mildly, to Toth he said, "I'll show you."

Bert passed his dagger from one hand to the other. "They're nothin' but thievin' bastards," he muttered.

"You're full of piss and wind, and you know it," Roland said. "Back off. If you're too afraid to go in, then get the Hell out of here."

Bert hesitated.

Roland looked up. "I said get the Hell out of here. The game is off. I ain't playing like you're boss no more. Back off."

Bert was slow to put the dagger away, but finally he did so and nodded. "Sure," he said. "This place just gets to me is all." He didn't make eye contact with Toth or Fretwell as he turned. He crunched through the snow and turned a corner. He waited with his back to them for a moment, as if poised to say or do something, but he thought better and went on.

"You had us fooled," Fretwell said. "It was a good act."

"Piss and wind," Roland said. The child craned his neck and looked up at Toth. The boy was only four feet tall. "Bert's a piss ant," he said. "No honor at all."

A little amazed, Toth said, "No, I suppose not." He side-eyed Fretwell.

"Relax. It's safer for me when you don't know who's in charge," Roland said. "Bert's just a stabber for me. He's got nary an ounce of brains. The boys call him Ethel, for God's sake. Hand over the lantern. I'll walk you through."

Fretwell handed over the light. Roland gripped the lantern and moved towards the grating. The metal groaned when he pulled it back. "You'll find it warmer down here," he said.

Toth, ducking, followed the boy into the darkness. Fretwell went last. He pulled the grating closed. The noise echoed through the long tunnel.

The candlelight made an orb that cut the darkness in a swath along the ground, while the uneven walls and sloping ceiling remained in shadow. Near the opening the stone was treacherous with half-melted snow, but ten feet within the ground was dry sand. With no wind the temperature began to rise.

When Roland spoke, even though he kept his voice to the register of a whisper, the words reverberated. "Here are the first hovels," he said. They had advanced no more than twenty feet inside the passageway. The child extended the light into the opening on their left. Toth peered inside. It was as Hyacinth had shown him. It was a man-made hole, the rock scraped away with hand tools, empty now of an inhabitant. A pile of rubbish waited in the corner. Water dripped loudly from the porous ceiling, making a puddle. The puddle had slush at its edge. This was a pitiful way for human beings to live, but it was better than the streets in winter. An equally forlorn hovel waited on the right side of the passage. Here there were burn marks against the wall—streaks of black. A family of rats recoiled at the intrusion of light. Their eyes went red, and they squealed.

The three passed twenty more such hovels before stopping, deep under the earth now, at an unexceptional hole cut into the right side of the passage. Little Roland turned with his light. A stray dog, its ribs exposed and belly bloated, a runt hound, had followed them from one of the earlier holes. The dog stood in their wake now, hopeful for an offering of food.

Roland ignored the animal. "This is the one," he said. "This is where Hyacinth lived. She was the only one who stayed this far down. Another thirty yards and you reach the grave pit. When the wind comes off the river, it'll carry the smell up this far. Not much farther."

This hovel was more complex and larger than the previous. It had, Toth guessed, been used for storage at some point in its history—maybe as something connected to the potter's field below. The design of the cave had an artistic flourish, as if care had gone into the crafting. A gnarled column, wet with condensation like a stalactite, braced the center. The walls around the column were rounded, creating the shape of a gourd. This cave, he sensed, was old enough to be from heathen times, a thousand years or more. It was the first cave cut after the grave pit, not the last in the sequence from above.

Fretwell stepped inside first. He kicked debris around and said, dejectedly, "There's nothing except ashes now."

It was true enough. Toth took the light from Roland and stepped inside. The pitiful hound followed, sniffing at the walls. The ceiling was low enough that Toth had to duck. Roland waited patiently in the main tunnel. He did not seem frightened, and he didn't seem curious. He was calm and collected, even though he stood alone in the dark.

Toth searched for several minutes, pushing through the ashes until soot covered his gloves and leather shoes. Nothing had been left intact. The destruction was thorough. He found tantalizing scraps of paper here and there, presumably the remnants of books, but fire left most of the writing illegible. He found the partial cover a printed book called *Fieldbook of Wound-Healing* by von Gersdorff, dated 1517. Apparently, there were people who visited Hyacinth for medicinal purposes. Enochian symbols, scratched into stone, marked the ceiling. Indeed, writing covered the walls and ceiling like latticework, but smoke damage obscured most of this. At the back of the cave, someone intentionally hacked away part of the ceiling, erasing something permanently, revealing the unblemished stone beneath. Bits of sand sparkled in the candlelight.

Roland, sensing Toth's disappointment, stepped out of the dark passageway and put a hand against the professor's arm. The hand was cold as ice, reminding him of the corpse that had entered his bed. "She called to you for a reason," the child said. He was sincere now—not irreverent, not tough. Being in the presence of this hovel seemed to have changed him. "We all have our duty to perform for her."

Toth caught a flash from the child's mind, but he scarce believed it. It was an image of creation, a memory of this hole in the earth. Toth straightened until his head bumped the ceiling. He raised the light until it fully revealed Roland's face. A wave of cold reached his heart. *She told us you would lead us*, he thought. *We followed you like she told us to do.*

Fretwell's reaction to Roland was more visceral. "What do you know of that?" he asked. He plowed through the ashes towards the opening of the cave. The hound jumped aside, lowering its head in fear at the sudden movement. Fretwell's voice was on the edge of panic, as if he'd come this far only to be trapped in a hole in the ground. Like a fool, he felt around for his dagger.

"All of it," Roland said. "Bring the light along. I need to show you something."

Again Toth glimpsed an abstract image of creation. He wondered if Fretwell experienced the same. He nodded at his companion, urging the man to be calm. This was no ordinary child. This was all part of Hyacinth's orchestration. All three were on a track she had created. If Roland had wanted to harm the men he would have done so already. He could've led the men into a deeper labyrinth. He could've allowed Bert to take a chance with the knife. Once he got beyond his frayed nerves, Fretwell knew this. He did his best to gather himself.

The two followed Roland out of the cave. They were descending now, more rapidly. Hovels no longer marred the walls. The desperate hound followed. What began as tendrils of decay, stray aromas, became a wave of dead flesh and offal. The stench grew into a miasmic cloud. It was enough to make one lurch. The passage narrowed, concentrating the wind from the holes below into a forceful lance. The passage also sloped at a dangerous grate, so much so that Toth and Fretwell had to hold their hands against the walls and ceiling to keep from falling. The lantern swung, the light tottered.

Roland stopped at a ledge. "You have to jump down from here," he said. At that, he leapt several feet to the ground. The thud of his landing resonated in the cavern. He reached up and took the lantern. He lit the ground. There were bones, animal and human alike, on the floor, gripped in a congealed layer of mud, decayed flesh, and rotten blood. Millions of healthy, fat rats nested in the bodies. Their collective noise of claw, teeth, and squeal made a nightmarish din in the cavern. The wind off the river, strong enough to lift hair on the uppermost corpses, competed for attention. Toth thought back to the Dutchmen in the coach and their talk of plague in Rotterdam. Plague looked like this. He'd never been inside such a pit, but he'd seen times when such graves were necessary. In what amounted to a self-mocking gesture, he covered his mouth.

The hound moved through Toth's legs and jumped downward. He went searching for food. He was still within the halo of Roland's light when he snapped at a slow rat and bit the rodent in half.

Toth and Fretwell took a seat on the edge of the stone, one after the other, and hopped down. An array of finger bones snapped like twigs under Fretwell's first step. He was nearly in shambles when his next step found the edge of a child's ribcage, breaking through the dusty chest. It was an ancient body with brittle, chewed-up bones, no flesh. Fretwell's face was bloodless.

Toth, seeing this, was more careful. He shuffled along the floor, pushing debris aside as he moved. His nerves, too, were busted now. His mind moved towards panic despite the effort to steel himself. He found it impossible to concentrate. He continued to cover his mouth and nose to filter the stench, but it was little help. The decay entered through pores.

The hound, apparently familiar with this feeding ground, climbed the mound of bodies, sniffing maniacally, biting here and there. A few cats, wary of the dog, remained still as statues in the dark.

The smells, sights, and sounds had no impact on Roland. He stood just as composed as he had been when he initially demanded money from Toth. He was a perfectly emotionless creature. Roland's shoes sunk into the flayed arm of a woman, a medical student's curiosity, but he seemed not to notice this either.

"Over here," he whispered. The boy walked over to a ledge against the far wall of the pit. The body of a child rested on the ledge in a sitting position. Someone had moved the body here, detached it from the mass of dead and arranged the limbs carefully. The cadaver looked poised to speak, almost alive it was so well preserved. Roland lifted the light as high as he could manage, standing on his toes to do so, and unveiled what he desired to show them.

Toth's breath caught. Blood drained from his features. Save for the waxen quality of the flesh, the face was the same. Down to the minutest detail, the face was that of Roland. The age, too, was the same. Absolutely everything. The day, from beginning to end, washed over him, and he stood in the tide of it, feeling battered. "What did she do?" Toth asked. He nearly grabbed the child by his collar and shook him. "What did she do?" he demanded.

Roland turned his light to the denser section of the pit—the horrid pile of flesh and bone. He said enough with the gesture. Here was the material of which he was made. Then he turned the light back to the sitting corpse. "She used the book," the boy said. "She mimicked this one." Then, casually, "There are others up top. Good ones. She drowned the bad ones in sacks in the river. The ones she could catch." He looked around the darkness then.

Toth did everything in his power to collect himself. Nature told him to panic and run. His stomach was sick, his nerves scissored. He turned and looked at Fretwell. The young man knelt at the ledge upon which the corpse child set. His head was down, his forearms draping his knees. His back heaved.

"The book's too valuable to lose," Roland said. "You've seen the fruit of its decipherment. It doesn't matter what you think of how she used it." Roland then did something that both fascinated and horrified Toth. He reached into the man's mind, made his presence known with the projection of a thought, and then he withdrew. It was a latent ability, weak and underdeveloped, but it was present nevertheless. *Hyacinth was becoming very skilled when she died*, the boy projected.

"You knew when I looked inside you," Toth said.

Roland nodded. "You saw the memory of this child." He pointed at the ledge. "Not mine. I can't disentangle them."

"Is Bert?"

"No, not him. There are only a few, and not all of them are children. She only mimicked people without families to notice, people in the caves. They won't be long. We deteriorate."

Presently, Fretwell stood. He wiped his hands against his cloak. Any emotion behind his eyes was shattered, but his face was set in grim determination. He'd see the thing through, but he wouldn't stand for idleness. "Where's the book?" he asked. He clenched his fists in an attempt to find strength. In the light, his hands were white as chalk.

"The book is still inside Hyacinth," Roland said. "She knew everything would be burned. She memorized the book before she died." Roland turned, looking past the mass of bodies to where the passage narrowed and sloped again. "It's out there with her now." He eyed Fretwell. "She knew of you in particular. She knew your grandfather once. He had a similar talent. She knew of both of you, knew your pedigrees." He looked at Toth. "Of your father, Almos Toth. He, too, had the ability."

"How?" Fretwell asked.

"She shared only what she needed to share with me," Roland said. "The book was very dear to her. She believed the two of you could recover it. That is all I know."

Toth watched Fretwell. He had reached into the mind of the dead, but it was not something with which one ever became familiar. The process was always different, and it was always dangerous. *Find strength*, he projected. *Your mind won't be able to stand it if you don't.*

The mass of bodies shifted, and a mix of bones cascaded down the side of one mound. Toth turned, expecting to see the dog rummaging, but the mutt was sitting on the ground, cleaning its crotch.

"It's best not to linger here," Roland said.

The passage to the river basin descended another thirty feet before leveling. At the end of the tunnel, the ceiling was no more than five feet from the ground. Toth and Fretwell stooped, but Roland walked upright. The hound had either remained behind in the grave pit or retreated to its original shelter. A metal grating, more solid than the one high above, separated this end of the passageway from the open field. The gate here, too, was not barred, but it was shut firmly against the stone. Wind rattled the bars. Roland pushed it open and stepped into the night air. Toth and Fretwell followed. The river air was a great relief, even if it smelled of fish and refuse. The odor of the cave had been traumatic.

"No more lantern," Roland said. "The magistrate could have a man on the wall." With a deft motion, he snuffed the candle. The lantern fell dark. Roland offered the lantern to Fretwell, but it was too hot to keep in a satchel. Fretwell placed it on the ground. He had no mind for possessions now. He had, Toth observed, become centered and focused. Toth had done his best to enter the same state. It was necessary to strip away all distractions at this juncture. Toth had been in the mind of the dead twice before, but only in search of simple things: ideas, names. He never faced the arduous task of siphoning an entire book. He questioned if he had the strength and ability to do so. Then he wondered at Fretwell's true strength, if he were a prodigy like his memories made claim.

"Follow me," Roland said.

The intensity of the snow grew while they were in the cave system. More than an inch covered the ground now, while fresh snow swirled in the air. The River Trent moved swiftly, its oily black current absorbing snow as it fell. The ground crunched as the three walked along the base of the cliff. Nottingham, crowned by its ruined castle, stood above, producing few points of light. Nothing stirred on Hethbeth Bridge. There was no sign of watchmen. The roads were empty.

Even without lantern or moonlight, one could spy the gallows. The structure rose from the ground like a lone tree. There were no birds now, as there had been during the light of day. Only the figure of Hyacinth, strange fruit at the end of a taut rope, decorated the gibbet. The corpse swayed in the wind. Snow covered her frozen hair and lined her withered shoulders. Her pitch-darkened face melded with the shadows.

Without ceremony, Roland walked straight to the body. He looked up, emotionless as an automaton. Hyacinth had been exposed to the elements for nearly a month. The hangman (a journeyman since a town like this would not payroll an executioner) had lathered the body thickly with pitch to slow decay and to keep birds from feeding. The cold and the pitch hastened a primitive mummification. The blackened skin was jarringly unnatural. The body remained here as a warning, a deterrent, the way pirates are strung up in metal cages at the Bristol docks. Hyacinth was the first thing to greet a traveler who crossed the bridge. *Such is the fate of the Devil's disciples*: that was the story the corpse told. If tradition served as a model, she would hang here until the sinew in her neck became too weak to hold weight and finally broke, separating head from body.

Being provincial, the town had largely left the corpse unmolested. In Dublin or London, a corpse such as this would be prey to necromancers and apothecaries. No obvious souvenirs had been cut from her flesh or clothing. No children had cut the twine holding shut the hem of her skirt. Her bare feet, black with pitch and frost, dangled beneath the end of the skirt. They had not been beaten or chewed or razored. Her gnarled hands were likewise preserved.

Toth looked into the face, at the cemented eyelids. No hood obscured Hyacinth's features. Pitch had congealed on her face to such an extent that the coating made a death mask. Her neck remained unbroken, so she had strangled to death. The mask preserved the anguish in her face, although her tongue did not protrude as one expected. It was not unusual for a person to bite off their tongue while strangling, and maybe Hyacinth had done so. The Puritans would have enjoyed a sight such as that. It was an image to toughen your children. Regardless, the mouth was a hard line now, shut forever.

Hyacinth, though, knew other ways to keep from being silenced. She understood the vegetable life a corpse held. She may have been uncouth, but she was not uneducated. Toth had heard of instances when life remained in a body for two months or more. Vegetable life was not a conscious existence, but it manifested worms and provided something of a pincushion for slivers of memory. A few nerves burned until the soul fully departed the shell. The Romani in Hungary knew this better than most. From childhood, Toth knew the tradition of leaving the dead out for weeks before burial to give the soul ample time to depart. Burying a corpse too soon risked trapping the soul eternally in the body. Premature burials, Romani warned in their folklore, created vampires.

Fretwell, who had been reverently silent, now spoke, "Dr. Toth, you don't know everything I've done."

Toth furrowed his brow.

Fretwell didn't meet his eyes. He turned and watched the river, looking past it. He went on. "I'll capture the book. You translate it."

"Why not the both of us?" Toth asked.

"It'll put me out for a few days. You'll need to watch over me. Who would watch over the both of us?" He looked at Roland, who stood at the feet of Hyacinth with his hands in his pockets. Now Fretwell projected rather than spoke. *I don't think the boy's life will be as long as you imagine. He was left behind for a purpose.* Then, after a moment, "I've done this before. Somehow she knew that."

Somberly, Toth nodded. It would be deceitful to say he was not relieved. The scheme of entering Hyacinth's mind terrified him. He could live with seeing the grimoire secondhand. The danger was not the book itself, but other stray thoughts that still quivered in the woman's mind. Fretwell would have to dig and explore, and he would not be shielded as he did so. If one absorbed the traumatic feeling of death, if the moment before dying was preserved, the effect could permanently wreck a mind. The task was a minefield.

Roland stepped forward. "Your dagger," he said. He put out his hand.

Fretwell offered the weapon.

Gripping the blade between his teeth, Roland approached the gallows. He nodded for Toth to follow. Toth understood. He lifted the child as high as he could manage. The cross beam of the gallows was about nine feet off the ground. Roland was oddly light. He grabbed hold of the beam. With a nimble effort, he pulled himself up, turned, and took a seat, straddling the rope. He sawed the hemp. The corpse fell to the ground in a heap, collapsing like a discarded sack.

Roland leapt downward, thumping hard against the ground. His leg, Toth saw, bent backwards in the fall, an unnatural and excruciating bow. Roland seemed unfazed. He handed the dagger back to Fretwell. When he turned, Toth saw that one of the child's leg bones had snapped, breaking through his skin and protruding from a rip in his trousers. Toth grew ill, but Roland felt nothing. The child peered upward at Nottingham with cat eyes. He was cautious and watchful.

What could he do, Toth wondered, *if he saw someone? He's deteriorating, coming apart.*

Toth pushed aside the distraction and placed his hand on Fretwell's back. He didn't have to say anything, but the two looked at one another for a moment. *You can trust me. I'll watch over you.*

I know you will. Fretwell handed over the dagger. "Just in case," he said.

Together, the men positioned Hyacinth's corpse until it was prostrate on the ground. Although unwieldy due to the ice and pitch, the corpse was neither brittle nor in a deep state of rigor mortis. Touching the body, though, was the equivalent of dipping a hand in freezing water. It was painfully cold, even through leather gloves. Toth moved aside Hyacinth's frozen hair. Strands snapped at the touch, and he couldn't help but to place a lock in his satchel. He took the opportunity, too, to looker closer at the face. There was agony in the lines, but there was also the courage not to demonstrate that agony. It was subtle suffering she had shown the people of Nottingham. She had not engaged in histrionics in her final moments, probably to the dismay of her audience. Although this was the face with which she'd threatened Toth in London, it wasn't horrible like his imagination fathomed. The sight brought more pity than revulsion.

Fretwell knelt. He began the process by digging his thumb into the pitch on Hyacinth's face, cracking it, removing shards. He wanted at the skin. Flesh came with the dried tar, exposing a layer of gray below. Fretwell moved his hands into the flesh.

With the dagger hidden in his coat, Toth stood. It was, he knew, a matter of waiting now. In his experience, the process of extraction could be tedious. Minutes passed. It was just as he gained his bearing that the metal grating downwind jostled. The noise was subtle, but the night was quiet enough that the intrusion grabbed his attention. Toth turned to look for Roland, thinking the boy had wandered back to the caverns. Instinctively, he removed the dagger from his coat. The weapon felt insubstantial in his hand, and he felt like a fool wielding it. Roland was not at the cavern gate. Rather, the child neared the riverbank, walking as if an unskilled puppeteer commanded his movements, moving steadily towards the water. He had mind enough to know he'd served his purpose. His work was done. It was fascinating to see the lack of ambition in a created thing.

She drowned the bad ones in sacks in the river, Roland had said. *The ones she could catch.*

Or the ones who obeyed, Toth thought, *simply self-exterminated.*

Roland waded into the icy water of the Trent. He did not turn back. He kept his face forward, his back to the city. He walked until he was fully submerged. The water carried away his hat. The snow-engorged current swept him under, and he was gone.

Toth didn't have time to be awed. In the distance, the gate opened.

Toth's pulse jumped. He looked back to check on Fretwell, who had now entered a blind state of trance, his hands spread on Hyacinth's half-exposed face. Grinding his teeth, Fretwell's face quaked at the jawline. He was searching, absorbing.

Toth strained to see in the darkness. He stepped towards the grating, shielding his face against the snow and wind. He held the dagger defensively at his stomach. Whatever it was, he had to protect Fretwell. The thought mortified him.

A dark shape, hunkered, emerged from the hole. At first, Toth believed the shape to be one of the children vagrants, possibly Ethelbert, who had followed through the catacomb. The movement was unnatural, though, painful. The body was broken. It was a small figure, that of a child. Despite this, the shape dragged something substantial behind it. When it reached the open air, the shape stood more erect, but a crooked spine limited the effect.

This, Toth thought, *is one of the ghosts that keep derelicts from living in the caves.*

The child-shape started towards him. In one hand, the androgynous thing gripped a stone. The stone had shadows on it like blood. With the other hand, the child gripped what remained of the stray hound. Blood and exposed bone rendered the dog unrecognizable, but it was too fresh to be anything else.

Toth positioned himself in front of Fretwell, gripping the dagger so tightly that he nearly twisted the handle. Any movement was difficult, an act of will. He felt locked to the ground, paralyzed.

This was one of Hyacinth's creations that did not obey. It ambled still closer. The action was thoughtless, funneled, just a drive to move forward and feed. It operated with insect impulse. The thing's rotten brain, whatever still fired inside it, produced nothing more than idiot chaos. The shell of the body had decayed to such a degree that the assemblage of parts was faltering, the bones falling inward on one another. The face was bloated with water, as if in a period of weakness, the thing had lain face down in a puddle until it regained strength. Rats had whittled the neck to the thinness of a scarecrow's limb. Blood covered the lipless mouth and exposed teeth.

Toth stepped back. The snow crunched. He didn't have the fortitude to step forward. Not now. He'd washed free the momentary paralysis, so it was difficult not to abandon Fretwell and run. Taking one step back was the most inoffensive way for his weakness to manifest.

The child-shape was within ten feet of him now. The thing struggled with the wind. The only noise it made was an intermittent drawing of breath, a quick and painful intake. The head shuddered every time the shape accomplished this action. The shape, a mocking inversion of Roland, stopped then. Only a few feet separated it and Toth. Through a set of fogged eyes, around which the muscles had fully collapsed, it peered at Toth and Fretwell, as if trying to decide a course of action. The child dropped the hound. Then, as the last of its strength drained, the shape went on its knees into the snow. A brittle bone snapped as it did so—like a tendon of ice breaking. The child toppled forward, planting its face downward in the snow.

Dear Jesus, Toth thought. His breathing was quick and shallow, emerging as wisps of frost. His heart beat a tattoo against his chest. The dagger trembled in his fist. He shoved the knife in his pocket. After several minutes, he inched forward. The child-shape did not move, although he had no doubt the thing was simply gathering its strength to move again. Such was its existence. Cautiously, Toth approached the miserable shape. The thing still held a stone in its hand, its grip like a bone claw.

Toth stood over the body. As he watched, fingers around the stone quivered, and a nail scratched into the sand. Toth, losing all inhibitions to the panic that overwhelmed him, lurched forward and stomped at the skull with all his weight. His mind went red. One savage blow from his heel and the bone caved like weak pottery, leaving the skull the shape of a crescent moon. He stomped until the head was an amorphous pile, coloring the snow.

Fretwell knew nothing of this. Undisturbed, he kept his hands upon Hyacinth's face. After he was certain Fretwell was fine, Toth managed to gather himself. The effort was imperfect and his calmness brittle, but he maintained a façade that reflected little of his inner lunacy. He waited there, standing above the child-shape and the poor hound, anticipating more movement at the cavern gate.

Nothing came. A gust of wind slammed the gate against the stone once, but nothing followed.

Satisfied that Fretwell would not be disturbed, Toth performed the odious task of dragging the child-shape to the river's edge. He made the long walk through the snow and returned to do the same with the hound. The blood froze against his gloves. He threw each corpse, the child first and then the dog, into the tide. Both floated on the current for several yards before sinking lower. Both were very light.

As Toth walked back to Fretwell and the gallows, he marveled about the possibilities of the grimoire like one marvels at a grotesque injury. A deep morbidity had to exist in Hyacinth to use the book to achieve these ends. *What else had her obsession wrought?*

Fretwell worked three more hours that night, while Toth paced to keep from freezing. Occasionally, the cavern gate would move with the wind, but not even a stray cat went in or out that he could see. Toth made himself useful by brushing snow from his companion and Hyacinth.

When Fretwell finished, the young man collapsed into the snow, which had gained three more inches since he'd begun. His skin was blue. Dawn was not far off. A purple tinged laced the horizon. Toth considered throwing Hyacinth into the river, too, to give her a burial, but the strength to do so simply wasn't there. He had to focus on Fretwell. Tapping his last reservoir of energy, Toth dragged Fretwell away from Hyacinth. With an effort that would permanently kink his spine, Toth lifted the man, cradling him across his arms, and started towards Hethbeth Bridge. Adrenaline and the fear of morning and being caught kept him moving.

Hyacinth remained behind, gathering snow.

Toth was taking his morning gin, a habit he'd formed over the past few months, when a knock rattled his door. He left Fretwell's side and the meager hearth, carrying his tin cup to the doorway. With a quick motion, he finished the drink.

The knocking kept up, hard.

Toth leaned against the planks. "We paid for a week," he said. There was only one side of a locked door upon which it was proper to argue with an innkeeper, and Toth occupied the correct side.

"Not the innkeeper," an unfamiliar voice replied. "It's the magistrate. Edmund Archer."

Toth glanced over his shoulder, scanning the room. When he was satisfied that his manuscripts were hidden (he'd yet to do much work this morning), he lifted the latch and pulled the door inward.

The magistrate stood in the narrow space at the top of the stairs. A large man with a great amount of fat around his neck and waist, he filled the space as completely as one man could. The curled wig he wore, which rose nearly a foot from the top of his head, added to his overbearing presence. He thought himself a magnificent figure, like little kings do. A look of vexation crossed his face. He eyed the red scarf around Toth's neck. "You are the gypsy, yes? The Hungarian?" he said. He put his foot on the threshold, as if he expected to have the door slammed in his face.

"Dr. Béla Toth, yes."

"Doctor of what, sir?"

"Theology. What is it that you want, magistrate?"

"Theology? Don't tell me you're Catholic." He scoffed.

"Not at all."

"What university did you attend?"

"Vienna."

"That is Catholic."

"What is it you want?" Toth asked, already exhausted by the human leech.

Archer forewent his prying and returned to the thing that vexed him. "A child came forward, a Bert Hallchurch, and he told a wicked little story about you and your companion. May I come in?"

Toth had prepared for this moment. In fact, he'd agonized over it. "I suspect you wouldn't want to come in. I fear my companion may have contracted plague, sir. I'm keeping him in this room until I know for certain."

Archer opened his mouth and raised his left eyebrow. The movement jostled the bangs of his wig. "Plague? You're joking."

"I hear it came north from Dover to London. A stage runs through here every few weeks, doesn't it?"

"I did hear the plague was rife in Rotterdam," Archer said. He thought to himself for a moment. The thought was unpleasant. "Let me see him."

Toth started to open the door further.

"On second thought, close the door and step out here," Archer said. "I won't taunt God or the Devil today."

Toth stepped out of the room and shut the door behind him. The space at the top of the stairs seemed miniscule now. He and Archer stood face to face. "What of this Bert Hallchurch?" Toth asked.

Archer covered his mouth and took a step backward, placing one foot on the descending stairs. Understandably, he looked torn. He'd lost any momentum he'd gained from pounding on the door. Regret creased his ample face. "The child said you and your companion did something to his friend. This other child, Roland was his name, hasn't been seen for three days."

"Did you know the boy?"

"Oh I don't know any of the urchins," Archer said. "I know them about as well as I know the cats in town. They come and go, of course. Master Hallchurch said this particular boy was a drifter with no roots here. He'd been in Nottingham no more than a year. The question is, do you know this child? This Roland? It'd be remiss not to ask."

Toth shook his head. "No, I'm afraid I don't. He's missing?"

"He's only missing. No foul play without a body, of course. He could've gone on to York or Manchester. It's cheap fare from here. Sometimes they even take the long walk."

"I'm sorry, magistrate. I don't know him. I did give some coins and food to vagrants when I first came to town."

"Oh, you did? We try not to encourage begging here. That's it then, I imagine. Those boys are setting you up as a mark. Tsk tsk. You fell for an act, sir." Archer started to go, but a higher power compelled him to ask, "What brought you here, Doctor?"

"Not the best time of year for it," Toth said, "but I wanted to see some of the country. I spoke at the Royal Society a couple weeks prior."

"Lord bless me, is that right? A Fellow, eh?"

"Not quite. Fretwell, my companion, is a student at Cambridge. I teach at Trinity in Dublin."

Incredulous, Archer said, "What say you take your aspirations and your budding plague and leave us in Nottingham be? There's a stage in the morning, sir. You do look like a Catholic, I must say."

"I'll leave when I know Fretwell's well," Toth said.

Archer turned away. "I'll be in touch if I hear anything more about young Master Roland. You'll do the same, won't you?"

Toth nodded, a meaningless gesture with Archer's back turned. The magistrate, unbothered, assumed acquiescence. The rotund man made his way down the stairs. He didn't look back, not even when he opened the door onto Hethbeth Bridge. He went out, his wig shaking.

When Toth reentered the room, he had a new sense of urgency. He moved towards the hearth and Fretwell. The man, as he had been for three days now, was in a state of semi-consciousness. Although he acknowledged little, he was able to take in water. He lay under blankets on a thin mattress of straw. His skin had lost its shade of blue.

Toth reached into his satchel and pulled out the manuscript for the *Grimoire of the Four Impostors*. Written in Enochian in his own hand, the book, he surmised, was nearly complete. There were four tales, each with an impostor at its core, each with a code waiting to be deciphered. Currently, he was transcribing the fourth and final tale, one of a traveling executioner.

Just a little more, he projected to Fretwell.

Fretwell stared towards the wooden beams of the ceiling. Even though it was day, early morning even, the fire was the only light in the room. There were no windows. Shadows from the hearth moved along the beams.

Toth concentrated. When he made a connection with Fretwell, he opened the book and started writing. He saw each symbol in his mind, just as Hyacinth had mem-orized the text. *We shall finish today*, he promised. *We're very close.*

Fretwell, in what was a pleasing sign, managed to nod. The look in his eyes said he was looking at this world, at the beams above him and at Toth's looming shadow, rather than at something more horrible in his mind's eye. The intensity had gone from his gaze. His lips no longer trembled. He had ceased grinding his teeth. *You're a prodigy, indeed,* Toth thought. *Damned strong, too.*

Toth wrote at a feverish pace, the scratch of his quill filling the room.

Finis

A NOTE ON THE TYPE

The text of this book is set in IM Fell Double Pica, and is a digitized version of a typeface comissioned by John Fell, (June 23, 1625–July 10, 1686) and created by Peter de Walpergen, a German type designer (1646–1703) who practised in Oxford.

"John Fell was an English bishop, academic and publisher who was dean of Christ Church Oxford. From 1666-1669 he served as the vice-chancellor of the University of Oxford and established the renowned Oxford University Press. The publishing house became one of Fell's favorite projects and engaged much of his energy and devotion. Fell was motivated to 'help pass on the knowledge and criticism that lived on the printed page.' Under his direction, the house published many classics of philosophy, philology and literature and the typography used in these early publications became known as the Fell types.

Fell developed these typefaces in their own workhouse with Peter de Walpergen as the type-founder. The style of the type was a hybrid of both Dutch and French which gives the type forms a visual personality that is quite unique. The Fell types fell out of favor with the advent of Dutch Caslon type and were unused for centuries."[1]

The Fell Types used in this book were digitally reproduced in 2004, by Igino Marini. *www.iginomarini.com*

1 *https://www.sessions.edu/notes-on-design/type-in-history-the-fell-types*

ABOUT THE AUTHOR

Coy Hall lives in West Virginia with his wife, and they share a home with their clumsy Great Pyrenees. Coy splits time as an author of horror and professor of history. History guides his writing, with most of his stories set in the past—sometimes the real past, sometimes an imagined one, but most often a mix of the two. Find out more about his stories and novels at www.coyhall.com.

NOSETOUCH PRESS ™

Nosetouch Press is an independent book publisher
tandemly based in Chicago and Pittsburgh.
We are dedicated to bringing some of today's most
energizing fiction to readers around the world.

Our commitment to classic book design in a digital
environment brings an innovative and authentic
approach to the traditions of literary excellence.

*The Nose Knows™

NOSETOUCHPRESS.COM

Horror | Science Fiction | Fantasy | Mystery
Supernatural | Gothic | Weird

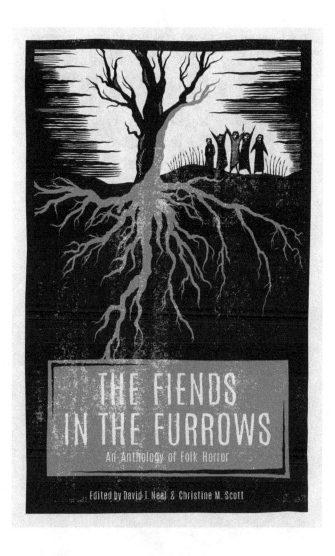

THE FIENDS
IN THE FURROWS

An Anthology of Folk Horror

Edited by David T. Neal & Christine M. Scott

Available in
PAPERBACK | HARDCOVER | EBOOK

NosetouchPress.com

Available in

PABERBACK | HARDCOVER | EBOOK

NosetouchPress.com

"This book is like a handful of crystals spread out across an altar, each blazing with its own color."
—Meg Elison, winner of the 2014 Philip K. Dick Award

SICTVS SVPERIVS,

WAX & WANE

A Gathering
of Witch Tales

ET INFERIVS

Edited by
David T. Neal *and* Christine M. Scott

Available in
PAPERBACK | EBOOK

NosetouchPress.com

CPSIA information can be obtained
at www.ICGtesting.com
Printed in the USA
LVHW090201141021
700408LV00004B/167